Loomis J. Campbell

Young Folks Book of Poetry

Containing a collection of the best short and easy poems for reading and recitation

in schools and families

Loomis J. Campbell

Young Folks Book of Poetry
Containing a collection of the best short and easy poems for reading and recitation in schools and families

ISBN/EAN: 9783337393861

Printed in Europe, USA, Canada, Australia, Japan

Cover: Foto ©Andreas Hilbeck / pixelio.de

More available books at **www.hansebooks.com**

YOUNG FOLKS'

BOOK OF POETRY

CONTAINING

A COLLECTION OF THE BEST SHORT AND EASY
POEMS FOR READING AND RECITATION
IN SCHOOLS AND FAMILIES

SELECTED AND ARRANGED

BY

LOOMIS J. CAMPBELL

———

BOSTON
LEE AND SHEPARD, PUBLISHERS
NEW YORK
CHARLES T. DILLINGHAM
1880

PREFACE.

THE First Part of this book is composed of Simple Poems which will be likely to interest and amuse young children who are not yet very expert in the art of reading. It is hoped that the selections will also foster a high moral tone of feeling, and yield an influence for right behavior and conduct.

The Select Poems in the Second and Third Parts are intended for children between the ages of eight or nine and thirteen or fourteen years. The plan of the book differs, in some respects, from that of any other collection which has come under the notice of the editor or compiler. The pieces are short and worthy of being committed to memory. They are also well fitted for reading aloud and for recitation.

It is needless to say that short poems of great excellence, sufficient in number to fill many volumes of the size of the present one, might have been easily found. The difficulty has been to select so small a quantity from the vast poetical wealth which has been accumulating for four hundred years. Unusual care, it is believed, has been taken to present only such poems as should be favorites in School and at Home. That a piece, when its merits were under consideration, should be true poetry, has been deemed of the first importance, and if, in any case, there has been a relaxing from a high poetic standard, it has been on account of some other excellence. Spirited rhetorical pieces fitted to instil into the minds of children right principles and sentiments, form a large proportion of the selections.

The editor would consider his work as wholly lost, if much the greater part of what is contained herein should not readily win the ear, and touch the heart, of the children into whose hands the book may come. The design has been to please its youthful readers, as well as to benefit them: hence cheerful and lively pieces have been especially sought. Even those poems containing a devotional element or flavor are not of a morbid cast, — such as declare this world a vale of tears, and depict this life as a misfortune which every good person rejoices to get rid of. Such poems have been chosen, rather, as speak of the world kindly, as a place where there are many beautiful things and many healthful pleasures to be seen and enjoyed. Thus we may teach faith and trust in the wise and good Father of all.

In the teaching of children there is danger, in this "eminently practical age," that the imagination will be too much neglected, and that they will lose something of great value, which cannot be made up to them by all the imperial bushels of facts which may be poured into them. The Fairies have fallen much into disrepute; the Cow no longer jumps *over* the moon; being a real graminivorous ruminating quadruped, she hardly jumps *under* it! Meanwhile is truth more honored in this age of gaslight and facts than in the darker age of rushlight and fancies?

The compiler wishes to say a good word for the practice of learning by heart. In what way can the taste be so well cultivated and refined, and the gentler feelings fostered, as by committing to memory a number of choice poems? The beauty of a true poem cannot be fully known until it is learned by heart. It is then ours, a companion and a joy forever, and, being interwoven with our earliest recollections, it grows more and more precious as we grow older. This, also, is something well worth doing, — to train and strengthen the memory in the period of life in which it may best be done.

When one of the poems has been selected for the class to learn by heart, the teacher should make sure that all the pupils thoroughly comprehend the piece. It is better to put them in the way of finding out for themselves than to give them the information. What is the main idea of the poem is a question which should be always asked. This main idea, or the general meaning, should be brought out so as to be clearly seen and realized.

After the text has been studied, and all difficulties are overcome, the poem may be correctly copied by each pupil, and then well learned by heart. In most cases, the latter part may be out-of-school work.

When the piece is publicly recited it should be done with feeling and effect. Attention should be paid to pronunciation, inflection, emphasis, etc.

Such selections as these may be used with great advantage in teaching young scholars the early steps of English composition. They may be required to write out the meaning of the poem in their own words, —to paraphrase it. Care should be taken that the ideas are correctly reproduced and in good form. The pupil should be taught not to be afraid to use the vocabulary which he already possesses. It is too much to expect him to furnish ideas: these come later on. Practice of this kind with the pen would be of much use where technical grammar, as now taught in most of the schools, is useless. It would be a help in teaching how to write one's native tongue.

L. J. C.

March, 1880.

CONTENTS.

The Three Parts are paged separately; hence the poem must be looked for in the Part and Page as here indicated; for example, to find the piece ABOU BEN ADHEM AND THE ANGEL . . . *Leigh Hunt* . . . 3 75 look in the Third Part and in Page numbered 75.

x CONTENTS.

FIRST

PART

I 'm a merry little maiden;
My heart is light and gay.

Poetry for Young Children.

✳ 1 ✳

LADY MOON. — A CHILD'S SONG.

> "I see the moon, and the moon sees me:
> God bless the moon, and God bless me."
>
> *Old Rhyme.*

LADY MOON, Lady Moon, where are you roving?
  Over the sea.
Lady Moon, Lady Moon, whom are you loving?
  All that love me.

Are you not tired with rolling, and never
  Resting to sleep?
Why look so pale and so sad, as forever
  Wishing to weep?

Ask me not this, little child, if you love me:
  You are too bold.
I must obey my dear Father above me,
  And do as I'm told.

Lady Moon, Lady Moon, where are you roving?
    Over the sea.
Lady Moon, Lady Moon, whom are you loving?
    All that love me.

RICHARD MONCKTON MILNES.
(LORD HOUGHTON).

* 2 *

THE NEW MOON.

O MOTHER, how pretty the moon looks to-night!
    She was never so cunning before:
Her two little horns are so sharp and so bright!
    I hope she'll not grow any more.

If I were up there with you and my friends,
    We'd [1] rock in it nicely, you'd [2] see;
We'd sit in the middle, and hold by both ends:
    Oh, what a bright cradle 'twould [3] be!

We'd call to the stars to keep out of the way,
    Lest we should rock over their toes;
And then we would rock till the dawn of the day,
    And see where the pretty moon goes.

And there we would stay in the beautiful skies,
    And through the bright clouds we would roam;
We'd see the sun set, and see the sun rise,
    And on the next rainbow come home.

MRS. FOLLEN.

---

[1] *we'd*, we would.   [2] *you'd*, you would.
[3] *'twould*, it would.

* 3 *

SPRING SONG.

THE spring is come!
The spring is come!
Again the earth rejoices;
  All streams and rills,
  And green-clad hills,
Lift up their cheerful voices.

The spring is come!
The spring is come!
The merry birds are singing;
  And in the grass,
  Where'er we pass,
The daisies white are springing.

The spring is come!
The spring is come!
The soft south wind is blowing;
  And in the dell [1]
  Where violets dwell,
We hear the brooklet [2] flowing.

* 4 *

THE CHILD'S MAY SONG.

A MERRY little maiden,
  In the merry month of May,
Came tripping o'er the meadow,
  As she sang this merry lay [3] : —

---

[1] *dell*, little valley.   [2] *brooklet*, little brook.
[3] *lay*, song.

"I'm a merry little maiden:
  My heart is light and gay;
And I love the sunny weather
  In the merry month of May.

"I love the pretty lambkins[1]
  That gayly sport and play,
And make such frolic gambols[2]
  In the merry month of May.

"I love the little birdies
  That sit upon the spray,[3]
And sing me such a blithe[4] song
  In the merry month of May.

"I love the blooming flowers
  That grow on bank and brae,[5]
And with them weave my garlands
  In the merry month of May.

"I love my little sisters
  And my brothers every day;
And I seem to love them better
  In the merry month of May."

---

[1] *lambkins*, little lambs.   [3] *spray*, small branch, sprig.
[2] *frolic gambols*, playful leaps.   [4] *blithe* (*th* as in *this*), joyful.
                [5] *brae*, slope of a hill.

* 5 *

THANK YOU, PRETTY COW.

THANK you, pretty cow, that made
Pleasant milk to soak my bread,
Every day and every night,
Warm and sweet, and fresh and white.

Do not chew the hemlock rank [1]
Growing on the weedy bank
But the yellow cowslips eat:
They will make it very sweet.

Where the bubbling water flows,
Where the purple violet grows,
Where the grass is fresh and fine,
Pretty cow, go there and dine.

JANE TAYLOR.

* 6 *

THE WIND.

I AM the wind,
    And I come very fast:
Through the tall wood
    I blow a loud blast.

Sometimes I am soft
    As a sweet, gentle child;
I play with the flowers,
    Am quiet and mild:

[1] *rank*, coarse, large.

And then out so loud
　　All at once I can roar;
If you wish to be quiet,
　　Close window and door.

I am the wind,
　　And I come very fast:
Through the tall wood
　　I blow a loud blast.

* 7 *

THE NORTH WIND.

THE north wind doth blow, and we shall have snow,
　　And what will the Robin do then, poor thing?
He'll sit in a barn,[1] and keep himself warm,
　　And hide his head under his wing, poor thing!

The north wind doth blow, and we shall have
　　　　snow;
　　And what will the Swallow do then, poor thing?
Oh! do you not know that he's gone long ago
　　To a country much warmer than ours? — poor
　　　　thing!

The north wind doth blow, and we shall have
　　　　snow;
　　And what will the Honey-bee do, poor thing?
In his hive he will stay till the cold's gone away,
　　And then he'll come out in the spring, poor
　　　　thing!

[1] The English robin stays in barns during winter; the American robin

The north wind doth blow, and we shall have
   snow;
  And what will the Dormouse[1] do then, poor
    thing?
Rolled up like a ball, in his nest snug and small,
  He'll sleep till warm weather comes back, poor
    thing!

The north wind doth blow, and we shall have
   snow;
  And what will the Children do then, poor
    things?
When lessons are done, they'll jump, skip, and
   run,
  And play till they make themselves warm, poor
    things!

GAMMER GURTON.

* 8 *

STOP, STOP, PRETTY WATER.

  " STOP, stop, pretty water!"
  Said Mary, one day,
  To a frolicsome brook
  That was running away.

  " You run on so fast!
  I wish you would stay:
  My boat and my flowers
  You will carry away.

---

[1] *dormouse*, an animal in England somewhat like the common mouse,
but larger. It remains torpid during winter.

" But I will run after, —
Mother says that I may, —
For I would know where
You are running away."

So Mary ran on ;
But I have heard say,
That she never could find
Where the brook ran away.

Mrs. Follen.

* 9 *

SLEEP, BABY, SLEEP!

Sleep, baby, sleep !
Thy father watches the sheep ;
Thy mother is shaking the dreamland tree,
And down comes a little dream on thee.
  Sleep, baby, sleep !

Sleep, baby, sleep !
The large stars are the sheep ;
The little stars are the lambs, I guess ;
And the gentle moon is the shepherdess.
  Sleep, baby, sleep !

Sleep, baby, sleep !
Our Saviour loves his sheep ;
He is the Lamb of God on high,
Who for our sakes came down to die.
  Sleep, baby, sleep !

From the German.

* 10 *

LULLABY.

Sweet and low, sweet and low,
  Wind of the western sea,
Low, low, breathe and blow,
  Wind of the western sea!
Over the rolling waters go,
Come from the dying moon, and blow,
  Blow him again to me;
While my little one, while my pretty one, sleeps.

Sleep and rest, sleep and rest,
  Father will come to thee soon;
Rest, rest, on mother's breast,
  Father will come to thee soon;
Father will come to his babe in the nest,
Silver sails all out of the west,
  Under the silver moon:
Sleep, my little one, sleep, my pretty one, sleep.

Alfred Tennyson.

* 11 *

BABY LAPP'S RIDE.

" Now give us a wrap,"
  Says the father Lapp,[1]
" And I'll take baby a ride to-day:

---

[1] *Lapp,* one who lives in Lapland, a cold country across the ocean, and
far up north.

Swiftly we'll go
Over the snow,
Ever and ever so far away ! "

So up in a wrap
They tuck little Lapp,
Till all you can see is baby's nose ;
And safe from harm,
On father's arm,
How loud and merrily baby crows !

For they're all the same,
Whatever their name,
Or whether at North or South they grow ;
They love to ride
By father's side
Whenever the ground is white with snow.

* 12 *

LITTLE RAIN-DROPS.

WHERE do you come from,
You little drops of rain,
Pitter-patter, pitter-patter,
Down the window-pane ?

They won't let me walk,
And they won't let me play,
And they won't let me go
Out of doors at all to-day.

They put away my playthings,
  Because I broke them all;
And then they locked up all my blocks,
  And took away my ball.

Tell me, little rain-drops,
  Is that the way you play, —
Pitter-patter, pitter-patter,
  All the rainy day?

They say I'm very naughty;
  Now I've nothing else to do
But sit here at the window;
  I should like to play with you.

The little rain-drops cannot speak;
  But "pitter-patter pat,"
Means, "We can play on *this* side,
  Why can't you play on *that?*"

AUNT EFFIE'S RHYMES.

* 13 *

THE LITTLE BOY AND THE STARS.

You little twinkling stars that shine
  Above my head so high,
If I had but a pair of wings,
  I'd join you in the sky.

If I were with you, little stars,
  How merrily we'd roll
Across the skies, and through the clouds,
  And round about the pole![1]

---

[1] *pole*, a point in the heavens near the north star.

The moon that once was round and full
   Is now a silver boat:
We'd launch it off the bright-edged cloud,
   And then — how we should float!

Does anybody say, " Be still,"
   When you would dance and play?
Does anybody hinder you,
   When you would have your way?

Oh tell me, little stars! for much
   I wonder why you go
The whole night long, from east to west,
   So patiently and slow."

" We have a Father, little child,
   Who guides us on our way:
We never question: 'when he speaks,
   We listen, and obey."

                        Aunt Effie's Rhymes.

* 14 *

BE POLITE.

Good boys and girls should never say,
   " I will," and " Give me these: "
Oh, no! that never is the way,
   But, " Mother, if you please."

And, " If you please," to sister Ann,
   Good boys to say are ready;
And, " Yes, sir," to a gentleman;
   And " Yes, ma'am," to a lady.

Hearts, like doors, can ope[1] with ease
  To very, very little keys;
And don't forget that two are these:
  " I thank you, sir," and, " If you please."

* 15 *

THE GOLDEN RULE.

DEAL with another as you'd have
Another deal with you:
What you're unwilling to receive,
Be sure you never do.

Be you to others kind and true,
As you'd have others be to you;
And neither do nor say to men
Whate'er you would not take again.

ISAAC WATTS.

* 16 *

WHICH LOVED BEST?

" I LOVE you, mother," said little John;
Then, forgetting his work, his cap went on,
And he was off to the garden swing,
And left her the water and wood to bring.

" I love you, mother," said rosy Nell, —
" I love you better than tongue can tell;" .
Then she teased and pouted full half the day,
Till her mother rejoiced[2] when she went to play.

---

      [1] *ope*, open.   [2] *rejoiced*, was glad.

"I love you, mother," said little Fan ;
"To-day I'll help you all I can :
How glad I am school doesn't[1] keep!"
So she rocked the babe till it fell asleep.

Then stepping softly she fetched the broom,
And swept the floor, and tidied[2] the room :
Busy and happy all day was she, —
Helpful and happy as child could be.

"I love you, mother," again they said,
Three little children going to bed :
How do you think that mother guessed
Which of them really loved her best?

JOY ALLISON.

* 17 *

IS IT YOU?

THERE is a child, a boy or girl, —
    I'm sorry it is true, —
Who doesn't[1] mind when spoken to :
    Is it? — it isn't you!
    Oh, no, it can't be you!

I know a child, a boy or girl, —
    I'm loath[3] to say I do, —
Who struck a little playmate child :
    Was it? — it wasn't you!
    I hope *that* wasn't you!

---

[1] *doesn't* (pronounced 'dŭznt').   [2] *tidied*, put it in good order.
[3] *loath*, unwilling.

I know a child, a boy or girl, —
  I hope that such are few, —
Who told a lie; yes, told a lie!
  Was it? — it wasn't you!
  It cannot be 'twas you!

There is a boy, — I know a boy, —
  I cannot love him, though, —
Who robs the little birdies' nests;
  Is it? — it can't be you!
  That bad boy can't be you!

A girl there is, — a girl I know, —
  And I could love her too,
But that she is so proud and vain:
  Is it? — it can't be you!
  That surely isn't you!
                    MRS. GOODWIN.

* 18 *

DON'T ROB THE BIRDS, BOYS.

DON'T rob the birds of their eggs, boys,
  It is cruel and heartless and wrong;
But remember, by breaking an egg, boys,
  We may lose a bird with a song.

When careworn, and weary, and lonely,
  Some day as you're passing along,
You'll rejoice that the egg wasn't broken
  That gave you the bird with its song.

* 19 *

THE ROBIN-REDBREASTS.

Two Robin-redbreasts built their nests
  Within a hollow tree;
The hen sat quietly at home,
  The cock sang merrily;
And all the little ones said,
  "Wee, wee, wee, wee, wee wee!"

One day, — the sun was warm and bright,
  And shining in the sky, —
Cock Robin said, " My little dears,
  'Tis time you learned to fly;"
And all the little ones said,
  "I'll try, I'll try, I'll try."

I know a child, — and who she is
  I'll tell you by and by, —
When mamma says, " Do this," or " that,"
  She says, " What for?" and " Why?"
She'd be a better child by far
  If she would say, " I'll try."

Aunt Effie's Rhymes.

* 20 *

THE OLD KITCHEN CLOCK.

  Listen to the kitchen clock!
To itself it seems to talk;
From its place it cannot walk:
  " Tick-tock tick-tock,"
    This is what it says.

" I'm a very patient clock;
Never moved by hope or fear,
Though I've stood for many a year;
' Tíck-tock tick-tock: ' "
This is what it says.

" I'm a very active clock,
For I go while you're asleep,
Though you never take a peep;
' Tick-tock tick-tock: ' "
This is what it says.

" I'm a very truthful clock;
People say about the place,
Truth is written on my face;
' Tick-tock tick-tock: ' "
This is what it says.

What a talkative old clock!
Let us see what it will do
When the pointer reaches two;
" DING DING ! — tick-tock: "
This is what it does.

* 21 *

THREE LITTLE CHICKS.

THREE little chicks so downy and neat
Went out in search of something to eat:
" Ter-wit, ter-weet !
Something to eat ! "
And soon they picked up a straw of wheat.

Said one little chick, "That belongs to me!"
Said one other little chick, "We'll see, we'll see!'
 "Ter-wit, ter-weet!
 It is nice and sweet,"
Said number three; "let us share the treat!"

They pulled and they tugged, the downy things,
And oh, how they flapped their baby wings!
 "Ter-wit, ter-weet!
 Something to eat!
Just please to let go of this bit of wheat!"

Fiercer and fiercer the battle grew,
Until the straw broke right in two.
 And the little chicks
 Were in a fix,
And sorry enough for their naughty tricks:

For a saucy crow has watched the fight,
And laughs, "Haw, haw! it serves you right!"
 So he snatches the prize
 From before their eyes,
And over the hills and away he flies!

* 22 *

THE MOTHER-BIRD.

"Peep, peep, peep!" says she;
"One, two, three, — one, two, three,
Little birds who wait for me.

" One is yellow, two are brown;
And their throats are soft with down:
On' each head a scarlet crown.

" Mother-bird is flying fast;
Soon your hunger will be past;
Here is mother come at last."

" Peep, peep, peep ! " says she ;
" Oh ! can it be? oh ! can it be?
No little ones here for me ! "

In vain her cry, in vain her quest:
A thoughtless boy had robbed her nest;
She looks around with aching breast.

FANNIE BENEDICT
(In " *The Nursery* ").

* 23 *

IF EVER I SEE—

IF ever I see
On bush or tree
Young birds in their pretty nest,
I must not in play
Steal the birds away,
To grieve their mother's breast.

My mother, I know,
Would sorrow so,
Should I be stolen away:
So I'll speak to the birds
In my softest words,
Nor hurt them in my play.

And when they can fly
In the bright blue sky,
They'll warble a song to me;
And then, if I'm sad,
It will make me glad
To think they are happy and free.

* 24 *

KINDNESS TO ANIMALS.

I WOULD not hurt a living thing,
However weak and small;
The beasts that graze,[1] the birds that sing, —
Our Father made them all:
Without his notice, I have read,
A sparrow cannot fall.

* 25 *

THE SNAIL.

THE Snail he lives in his hard round house,
In the orchard, under the tree:
Says he, " I have but a single room;
But it's large enough for me."

The Snail in his little house doth dwell
From week's end to week's end:
You're at home, Master Snail; that's all very well,
But you never receive a friend.

---

[1] *graze*, eat grass.

* 26 *

LITTLE STAR.

TWINKLE, twinkle, little star!
How I wonder what you are,
Up above the world so high,
Like a diamond in the sky!

When the glorious sun is set,
When the grass with dew is wet,
Then you show your little light,
Twinkle, twinkle, all the night.

In the dark blue sky you keep,
And often through my curtains peep;
For you never shut your eye
Till the sun is in the sky.

As your bright and tiny[1] spark
Lights the traveller in the dark,
Though I know not what you are,
Twinkle, twinkle, little star!

* 27 *

GOD IS GOOD AND KIND.

How very kind is God to me!
Look where I may, his gifts I see;
The food I eat, the clothes I wear,
Are tokens of my Maker's care.

---

[1] *ti'ny*, little.

He guards me both by day and night;
It is his sun that gives me light;
And, while in sleep my rest I take,
He keeps me safe until I wake.

When I am ill, he knows my pain,
And often makes me well again :
When I am well, he keeps me so;
And all I have to him I owe.

He gives me friends and teachers kind,
Who seek to train my infant mind
His holy name to know and love,
And raise my thoughts to things above.

Lord, let thy tender love to me
Draw forth my heart in love to thee, —
Love that shall lead me to obey
And serve and praise thee day by day.

J. BURTON.

* 28 *

GOD'S CARE OF ANIMALS.

WHO taught the bird to build her nest
    Of wool and hay and moss?
Who taught her how to weave it best,
    And lay the twigs across?

Who taught the busy bee to fly
    Among the sweetest flowers,
And lay her store of honey by
    To eat in winter hours?

Who taught the little ant the way
  Her narrow hole to bore,
And through the pleasant summer day
  To gather up her store?

'Twas God who taught them all the way,
  And gave their little skill;
He teaches children, when they pray,
  To do his holy will.

JANE TAYLOR.

* 29 *

WHAT A CHILD HAS.

I HAVE two eyes so bright and clear,
And they see things afar and near, —
The bird, the tree, the flower so small,
And the blue sky, bent over all.

Two ears have I upon my head,
For me to hear what may be said;
To hear my mother's words so mild, —
" Be good and gentle, my dear child!"

I have one mouth, as all may see;
But well its use is known to me;
For I can talk with it all day,
And all that I may think can say.

I have two hands so soft and white, —
This is the left, and this the right, —
Five little fingers stand on each,
With which to hold, to feel, and reach;

But, when I grow as tall as you,
A deal of work they then will do.

I have two feet at my command,
With which to walk, or run, or stand;
And should I tumble down — why, then
I must with speed jump up again.
But, when I grow both large and strong,
I shall quite boldly march along.

* 30 *

HOURS SPENT ARIGHT.

THE morning hours of cheerful light,
  Of all the day, are best;
But, as they speed their hasty flight,
If every hour is spent aright,
We sweetly sink to sleep at night,
  And pleasant is our rest.

And life is like a summer day,
  It seems so quickly past:
Youth is the morning bright and gay;
And, if 'tis spent in wisdom's way,
We meet old age without dismay,
  And death is sweet at last.

* 31 *

THE DARLING LITTLE GIRL.

WHO's the darling little girl
   Everybody loves to see?
She it is whose sunny face
   Is as sweet as sweet can be.

Who's the darling little girl
   Everybody loves to hear?
She it is whose pleasant voice
   Falls like music on the ear.

Who's the darling little girl
   Everybody loves to know?
She it is whose acts and thoughts
   All are pure as whitest snow.

* 32 *

LITTLE WHITE LILY.

LITTLE white Lily
   Sat by a stone,
Drooping and waiting
   Till the sun shone.
Little white Lily
   Sunshine has fed;
Little white Lily
   Is lifting her head.

Little white Lily
  Said, " It is good,
Little white Lily's
  Clothing and food." .
Little white Lily,
  Dressed like a bride,
Shining with whiteness,
  And crownèd beside !

Little white Lily
  Droopeth with pain,
Waiting and waiting
  For the soft rain.
Little white Lily
  Holdeth her cup ;
Rain is fast falling, ·
  And filling it up.

Little white Lily
  Said, " Good again,
When I am thirsty
  To have nice rain ;
Now I am stronger,
  Now I am cool ;
Heat cannot burn me,
  My veins are so full."

Little white Lily
  Smells very sweet ;
On her head sunshine,
  Rain at her feet.

* 35 *

TWO AND ONE.

Two *ears* and only *one mouth* have you:
  The reason, I think, is clear:
It teaches, my child, that it will not do
  To *talk* about all you *hear.*

Two eyes and only *one mouth* have you:
  The reason of this must be,
That you should learn that it will not do
  To *talk* about all you *see.*

Two hands and only *one mouth* have you;
  And it is worth repeating, —
The *two* are for work you will have to do,
  The *one* is enough for eating.

From the German.

* 36 *

LORD AND LADY ROBIN.

"Chirp! chipper! twitter! trill!"
  All on the morn of May
Lord and Lady Robin were out,
  So brave [1] in their scarlet and gray,
Fain to spy [2] what spot might be best
For building their palace that we call a nest.

"Chirp! chipper! twitter! trill!"
  "*Here,* oh, *here* let it be!
White blossoms and red fruit
  Will come to the cherry-tree."

[1] *brave,* bold, fearless; *here,* showy, beautiful.
[2] *fain to spy,* glad to see or find.

" *There*, oh, *there*, in yon maple high!
Near, so near, to the bright blue sky!"

"Chirp! chipper! twitter! trill!"
  Loud and fast and long;
Sweetest wrangle ever heard,
  For it was all in song.
And the spot Lord and Lady Robin liked best,
You will know by and by, when you see the nest.

Emily A. Braddock.

* 37 *

THE MICE.

The merry mice stay in their holes,
  And hide themselves by day;
But, when the house is still at night,
  The rogues come out to play.

They climb upon the pantry shelf,
  And taste of all they please;
They drink the milk that's set for cream,
  And nibble bread and cheese.

But, if they chance to hear the cat,
  Their feast will soon be done:
They'll scamper off to hide themselves
  As fast as they can run.

Some tiny mice live in the fields,
  And feed on flies and corn;[1]
And in a pretty hanging-nest
  The little ones are born.

[1] *corn*, here means "grains of wheat, rye, barley," etc.

When winter comes, they burrow holes,
    And line them soft with hay;
And, while the snow is on the ground,
    They sleep the time away.

. All living creatures like to be
    As free as you and I:
They love the fields, the woods, and hills,
    They love the sweet blue sky.

* 38 *

WHAT THE WINDS BRING.

" Which is the wind that brings the cold?"
  " The North wind, Freddy, and all the snow;
And the sheep will scamper into the fold
    When the North begins to blow."

" Which is the wind that brings the heat?"
  " The South wind, Katie; and corn will grow,
And peaches redden, for you to eat,
    When the South begins to blow."

" Which is the wind that brings the rain?"
  " The East wind, Arty; and farmers know
That cows come shivering up the lane
    When the East begins to blow."

" Which is the wind that brings the flowers?"
  " The West wind, Bessy; and soft and low
The birdies sing in the summer hours
    When the West begins to blow."

EDMUND C. STEDMAN.

* 39 *

CHOICE STANZAS.

Do you know how many children
Go to little beds at night,
Sleeping there so warm and cosey [1]
Till they wake with morning light?
God in heaven each name can tell,
Knows them all, and loves them well.

LET all your work be early done:
By lazy sloth [2] no prize is won,
And time and tide will wait for none.

THE moments fly, a minute's gone;
The minute's fly, an hour is run;
The day is fled, the night is here;
Thus flies a week, a month, a year.

SPEAK the truth, and speak it ever,
    Cost it what it will:
He who hides the wrong he did
    Does the wrong thing still.

---

[1] *cosey*, comfortable.
[2] *sloth* (from *slow*, and pronounced 'slōwth'), laziness.

**
***

KIND hearts are the gardens,
Kind thoughts are the roots,
Kind words are the blossoms,
Kind deeds are the fruits.

**
***

I WOULD not be a cruel boy
  For all that this world gives,
I would not take a single joy
  From any thing that lives.

**
***

WHATEVER brawls disturb the street,
  There should be peace at home;
Where sisters dwell, and brothers meet,
  Quarrels should never come.

**
***

Do something for each other,
  Though small the help may be;
There's comfort oft in little things,
  Far more than others see.

**
***

WHEN Work comes into a house to stay,
Then Want will speedily flee away;
But let Master Work once go to sleep,
And Want will in at the window peep.

* 40 *

THE SHOWER.

HEAR the rain, patter, patter,
Beat the pane, clatter, clatter!
Down it pours, helter, pelter;
Quick indoors! shelter, shelter!
See it rush, and roar and whirl,
Fight and push, eddy and swirl,[1]
Through the street, down the gutters!
Hear it beat 'gainst the shutters
In its grief and wild despair!
But 'tis brief, and we don't care:
We don't care, for, peeping through,
We see there two bits of blue;
And the sun, in spite of rain,
Has begun to smile again.

* 41 *

THE WAVES ON THE SEA–SHORE.

ROLL on, roll on, you restless waves
    That toss about and roar:
Why do you all run back again
    When you have reached the shore?

Roll on, roll on, you noisy waves;
    Roll higher up the strand:[2]
How is it that you cannot pass
    That line of yellow sand?

---

[1] *swirl*, whirl.   [2] *strand*, beach, shore.

Make haste, or else the tide will turn;
  Make haste, you noisy sea!
Roll quite across the bank, and then
  Far on across the lea.[1]

" We must not dare," the waves reply:
  " That line of yellow sand
Is laid along the shore to bound
  The waters and the land:

" And all should keep to time and place,
  And all should keep to rule, —
Both waves upon the sandy shore,
  And little boys at school."

AUNT EFFIE'S RHYMES.

* 42 *

AN OLD GAELIC CRADLE-SONG.

HUSH! the waves are rolling in,
  White with foam, white with foam:
Father toils amid the din;
  But baby sleeps at home.

Hush! the winds roar hoarse and deep,
  On they come, on they come!
Brother seeks the lazy sheep,
  But baby sleeps at home.

Hush! the rain sweeps o'er the knowes,[2]
  Where they roam, where they roam:
Sister goes to seek the cows;
  But baby sleeps at home.

---

[1] *lea*, grass-land.
[2] *knowes* (pronounced to rhyme with 'cows'), knolls, low hills.

* 43 *

WHAT DOES LITTLE BIRDIE SAY?

WHAT does little birdie say
In her nest at peep of day?
"Let me fly," says little birdie;
"Mother, let me fly away."
Birdie, rest a little longer,
Till thy little wings are stronger.
So she rests a little longer,
Then she flies away.

What does little baby say
In her bed at peep of day?
Baby says, like little birdie,
"Let me rise, and fly away."
Baby, sleep a little longer,
Till thy little limbs are stronger.
If she sleeps a little longer,
Baby too shall fly away.

ALFRED TENNYSON.

* 44 *

THE HOLIDAY.

COME out, come out, for merry play:
This is the pleasant month of June,
And we will go this afternoon
Over the hills and far away.

Hurrah! we'll have a holiday;
And through the wood, and up the glade,[1]
We'll go, in sunshine and in shade,
Over the hills and far away.

The wild rose blooms upon the spray;[2]
In all the sky is not a cloud;
And merry birds are singing loud,
Over the hills and far away.

Not one of us behind must stay;
But little ones and all shall go,
Where summer breezes gently blow,
Over the hills and far away.

MRS. HAWTREY.

* 45 *

SNOW.

SNOW, snow, everywhere! —
On the ground and in the air,
In the fields and in the lane,
On the roof and window-pane.

Snow, snow, everywhere!
Making common things look fair, —
Stones beside the garden walks,
Broken sticks, and cabbage stalks.

Snow, snow, everywhere!
Dressing up the trees so bare,

---

[1] *glade*, an open place in a wood.   [2] *spray*, a sprig, or small branch.

Resting on each fir-tree bough,
　Till it bends, a plume of snow.

Snow, snow, everywhere!
Covering up young roots with care,
Keeping them so safe and warm,
Jack Frost cannot do them harm.

Snow, snow, everywhere!
We are glad to see it here:
Snowball making will be fun
When to-morrow's work is done.

* 46 *

THE HOLIDAYS.

FAREWELL to study and to books;
　How fast the time is winging!
We soon shall to the woods away,
　And with the birds be singing.

We hail again this joyous day,
　For we are tired and weary;
The schoolroom, with its daily toil,
　Is getting dull and dreary.

We'll roam among the bright green fields,
　Where woods and flowers are springing,
And where the sturdy husbandman [1]
　The harvest home is bringing.

---

[1] *husbandman*, farmer.

And when the holidays are o'er
We'll have a joyous meeting;
When teachers, schoolmates, back shall come
With each a happy greeting.

* **47** *

WISHING.

RING-TING! I wish I were a Primrose,
A bright yellow Primrose blowing in the spring!
The stooping bough above me,
The wandering bee to love me,
The fern and moss to creep across,
And the Elm-tree for our king!

Nay, — stay! I wish I were an Elm-tree,
A great lofty Elm-tree, with green leaves gay!
The winds would set them dancing,
The sun and moonshine glance in,
And birds would house [1] among the boughs,
And sweetly sing.

Oh, no! I wish I were a Robin, —
A Robin, or a little Wren, everywhere to go,
Through forest, field, or garden,
And ask no leave or pardon,
Till winter comes with icy thumbs
To ruffle up our wing!

Well, — tell! where should I fly to,
Where go sleep in the dark wood or dell?

[1] *house,* make their nests.

Before the day was over,
Home must come the rover,
For mother's kiss, — sweeter this
Than any other thing.

WILLIAM ALLINGHAM.

* 48 *

THANKSGIVING-DAY.

OVER the river, and through the wood,
To grandfather's house we go;
The horse knows the way
To carry the sleigh
Through the white and drifted snow.

Over the river, and through the wood;
Oh, how the wind does blow!
'It stings the toes,
And bites the nose,
As over the ground we go.

Over the river, and through the wood,
And straight through the barnyard gate;
We seem to go
Extremely slow;
It is so hard to wait!

Over the river, and through the wood;
Now grandmother's cap I spy!
Hurrah for the fun!
Is the pudding done?
Hurrah for the pumpkin-pie!

LYDIA MARIA CHILD.

* 49 *

THE BUSY BEE.

How doth the little busy bee
  Improve each shining hour,
And gather honey all the day
  From every opening flower!

How skilfully she builds her cell!
  ·How neat she spreads the wax!
And labors hard to store it well
  With the sweet food she makes.

In works of labor or of skill
  I would be busy too;
For Satan finds some mischief still
  For idle hands to do.

In books, or work, or healthful play,
  Let my first years be passed,
That I may give for every day
  Some good account at last.

ISAAC WATTS.

* 50 *

THE BEE.

I LOVE to see
  The busy bee;
I love to watch the hive;
  When the sun's hot,
  They linger not:
It makes them all alive.

God gave them skill,
And with good will
They to their work attend:
Each little cell
Is shaped so well,
That none their work can mend.

Now in, now out,
They move about,
Yet all in order true:
Each seems to know
Both where to go
And what it has to do.

Midst summer heat,
The honey sweet
It gathers while it may,
In tiny drops,
And never stops
To waste its time in play.

I hear it come;
I know its hum:
It flies from flower to flower,
And to its store
A little more
It adds each day and hour.

Just so should I
My heart apply
My proper work to mind;

Look for some sweet
In all I meet,
And store up all I find.

* 51 *

THE MAIDEN AND THE BIRD.

"Little bird, little bird, come to me!
I have a green cage all ready for thee;
Beauty-bright flowers I'll bring anew,
And fresh ripe cherries all wet with dew."

"Thanks, little maiden, for all thy care;
But I dearly love the clear, cool air,
And my snug little nest in the old oak-tree."
"Little bird, little bird, stay with me!"

"Nay, little damsel,[1] away I'll fly
To greener fields and a warmer sky:
When spring returns with pattering rain,
You'll hear my merry song again."

"Little bird, little bird, who'll guide thee
Over the hills and over the sea?
Foolish one, come, in the house to stay;
For I'm very sure you'll lose your way."

"Ah, no, little maiden! God guides me
Over the hills and over the sea:
I will be free as the rushing air,
And sing of sunshine everywhere."

LYDIA MARIA CHILD.

¹ *damsel,* girl, maiden.

* 52 *

THE BOY AND THE SHEEP.

"LAZY sheep, pray tell me why
In the pleasant field you lie,
Eating grass and daisies white,
From the morning till the night:
Every thing can something do;
But what kind of use are you?"

"Nay, my little master, nay,
Do not serve me so, I pray!
Don't you see the wool that grows
On my back to make your clothes?
Cold, ah, very cold you'd be,
If you had not wool from me.

"True, it seems a pleasant thing
Nipping daisies in the spring;
But what chilly nights I pass
On the cold and dewy grass,
Or pick my scanty dinner where
All the ground is brown and bare!

"Then the farmer comes at last,
When the merry spring is past,
Cuts my woolly fleece away,
For your coat in wintry day.
Little master, this is why
In the pleasant fields I lie."

ANN TAYLOR.

* 53 *

STARS.

How pretty is each little star,
  Each tiny twinkler, soft and meek !
Yet many in this world there are
  Who do not know that stars can speak.

To them the skies are meaningless,
  A star is not a living thing ;
They cannot hear the messages
  Those shining creatures love to bring.

Hush ! listen ! ah, it will not do ;
  You do but listen with your ears ;
And stars are understood by few,
  For it must be the heart that hears.

Look up, not *only* with your eyes ;
  Ah ! do you hear a tender sound ?
To hearts familiar with the skies,
  The stars are nearer than the ground.

POEMS FOR A CHILD.

* 54 *

PERSEVERE.

THE fisher who draws in his net too soon
  Won't have any fish to sell:
The child who shuts up its book too soon
  Won't learn any lessons well.

1 *sluggard,* lazy person.

For if you would have your learning stay
   Be patient, don't learn too fast:
The man who travels a mile each day
   Will get round the world at last.
               H. W. DULCKEN. — *From the German.*

* 55 *

THE POND AND THE BROOK.

"Neighbor Brook," said the Pond one day,
"Why do you flow so fast away?
Sultry June is hastening on,
And then your water will all be gone."

"Nay, my friend," the Brook replied,
"Do not thus my conduct chide:
Shall I rather hoard[1] than give?
Better die than useless live."

Summer came, and blazing June
Dried the selfish Pond full soon;
Not a single trace was seen
Where it had so lately been.

But the Brook with vigor flowed
Swift along its pebbly road;
And the fragrant flowers around
Loved to hear its happy sound.

       [1] *hoard*, store up secretly.

Who made the moon and stars so high,
The darksome[1] night to cheer,
That shine so bright in yonder sky,
Oft as the heavens are clear?

Who made the rocks, the hills, the trees,
The mountains, and the vales?
The flocks, the herds, the cooling breeze,
The stream that never fails?

'Twas God who made this world so fair,
The shining sun, the sky, the air;
'Twas God who made the sea, the ground,
And all the things I see around.

* 58 *

THE LAMB.

LITTLE Lamb, who made thee?
Dost thou know who made thee?
Gave thee life, and bade thee feed
By the stream and o'er the mead?[2]
Gave thee clothing of delight, —
Softest clothing, woolly, bright?
Gave thee such a tender voice,
Making all the vales rejoice?
Little Lamb, who made thee?
Dost thou know who made thee?

---

[1] *darksome*, dark, gloomy   [2] *mead*, meadow, grass-land.

Little Lamb, I'll tell thee;
Little Lamb, I'll tell thee.
He is callèd by thy name,
For He calls Himself a Lamb : —
He is meek, and He is mild;
He became a little child :
I, a child, and thou, a lamb,
We are callèd by His name.
> Little Lamb, God bless thee !
> Little Lamb, God bless thee !

W. BLAKE.

* 59 *

TO A REDBREAST.

LITTLE bird, with bosom red,
Welcome to my humble shed;
Daily near my table steal,[1]
While I pick my scanty meal;
Doubt not, little though there be,
But I'll cast a crumb to thee,
Well rewarded if I spy
Pleasure in thy glancing eye;
See thee, when thou'st[2] eat thy fill,
Plume[3] thy breast, and wipe thy bill.
Come, my feathered friend, again !
Well thou know'st the broken pane : —
Ask of me thy daily store,
Ever welcome to my door.

J. LANGHORNE.

[1] *steal*, come quietly.
[2] *thou'st*, thou hast.
[3] *plume*, to pick and adjust the feathers.

The skies are dimming; the birds fly low,
Skimming and swimming, their wings are slow;
They float, they are carried, they scarcely go.

The dead leaves hurry; the waters, too,
Flurry and scurry, as if they knew
A storm was at hand; the smoke is blue.

LILLIPUT LEVEE.

* 64 *

THE WATCH-DOG.

" Bow, wow, wow! "
'Tis the great watch-dog,
  I know by his honest bark:
" Bow, wow, wow! "
Says the great watch-dog
  When he hears a foot in the dark.

Not a breath can stir
But he's up with a whir,[1]
  And a big bow-wow gives he;
And, with tail on end,
He'll the house defend
  Far better than lock or key.

When we sleep sound,
He takes his round,
  A sentry[2] o'er us all:

---

[1] *whir*, whirl, a turning about quickly.
[2] *sentry*, soldier on guard.

Through the long dark night,
Till broad daylight,
 He scares the thieves from the wall.

But through the whole day
With the children he'll play,
 And gambol[1] in the sun;
On his back astride
They may safely ride,
 For well he loves their fun.

By all he's known
To be true to the bone;[2]
 No flattering tongue has he;
And we may all learn
From the great watch-dog
 Both faithful and fond to be.

A. SMART.

✱ 65 ✱

THE CLUCKING HEN.

" WILL you take a walk with me,
 My little wife, to-day?
There's barley in the barley field,
 And hay-seed in the hay."

" Oh, thank you!" said the clucking hen;
 " I've something else to do;
I'm busy sitting on my eggs;
 I cannot walk with you."

---

[1] *gambol*, frisk, sport.
[2] thoroughly faithful, — to the backbone, as it were.

"Cluck, cluck, cluck, cluck!"
  Said the clucking hen;
"My little chicks will soon be hatched;
  I'll think about it then."

The clucking hen sat on her nest, —
  She made it in the hay, —
And warm and snug beneath her breast
  A dozen white eggs lay.

"Crack, crack!" went all the eggs;
  Out dropped the chickens small.
"Cluck!" said the clucking hen;
  "Now I have you all.

"Come along, my little chicks,
  I'll take a walk with *you*."
"Hollo!" said the barn-door cock;
  "Cock-a-doodle-doo!"
                    AUNT EFFIE'S RHYMES.

* 66 *

FREDDIE AND THE CHERRY-TREE.

FREDDIE saw some fine ripe cherries
  Hanging on a cherry-tree,
And he said, "You pretty cherries,
  Will you not come down to me?"

"Thank you kindly," said a Cherry;
  "We would rather stay up here:
If we ventured down this morning,
  You would eat us up, I fear."

One — the finest of the cherries —
  Dangled from a slender twig:
" You are beautiful," said Freddie;
  " Red and ripe, and, oh, how big!"

" Catch me," said the Cherry, " catch me,
  Little master, if you can!"
" I would catch you soon," said Freddie,
  " If I were a grown-up man."

Freddie jumped, and tried to reach it,
  Standing high upon his toes;
But the Cherry bobbed about,
  And laughed, and tickled Freddie's nose.

" Never mind!" said little Freddie,
  " I shall have them when it's right:"
But a Blackbird whistled boldly,
  " I shall eat them all to-night."

                    AUNT EFFIE'S RHYMES.

* 67 *

THE ANT AND THE CRICKET.

A SILLY young Cricket, accustomed to sing
Through the warm sunny months of the summer
            and spring,
Began to complain when he found that at home
His cupboard[1] was empty, and winter was come.
        Not a crumb to be found
        On the snow-covered ground;

---

[1] *cupboard* (pronounced ' kub'burd').

Not a flower could he see,
Not a leaf on a tree:
"Oh! what will become," said the Cricket, "of
    me?"

At last, by starvation and famine made bold,
All dripping with wet, and trembling with cold,
Away he set off to a miserly Ant,
To see if, to keep him alive, he would grant
    A shelter from rain,
    And a mouthful of grain.
    He wished only to borrow,
    And repay it to-morrow;
If not, he must die of starvation and sorrow.

Said the Ant to the Cricket, "I'm your servant and
    friend;
But we ants never borrow, we ants never lend.
But tell me, dear sir, did you lay nothing by
When the weather was warm?" Said the Cricket,
    "Not I!
    My heart was so light
    That I sang day and night,
    For all nature looked gay."
    "You sang, sir, you say?
Go then," said the Ant, "and dance winter away."
Thus ending, he hastily opened the wicket,
And out of the door turned the poor little Cricket.

Though this is a fable, the moral is good:
If you live without work, you will go without
    food.

* 68 *

THE WASP AND THE BEE.

A wasp met a bee that was just buzzing by,
And he said, " Little cousin, can you tell me why
You are loved so much better by people than I?

"My back shines as bright and as yellow as gold,
And my shape is most elegant, too, to behold;
Yet nobody likes me for that, I am told."

"Ah, cousin!" said the bee, "'tis all very true;
But if I were half as much mischief to do,
Indeed they would love me no better than you.

" You have a fine shape, and a delicate[1] wing;
They own you are handsome: but then there's one
        thing
They cannot put up with — and that is your sting.

" My coat is quite homely and plain, as you see,
Yet nobody ever is angry with me,
Because I'm a harmless and diligent bee."

From this little story, let people beware;
Because, like the wasp, if ill-natured they are,
They will never be loved, though ever so fair.

[1] *delicate,* slight and pretty.

* 69 *

TELL ME WHAT THE MILL DOTH SAY.

TELL me what the mill doth say:
"Clitter, clatter," night and day;
When we sleep, and when we wake,
Clitter, clatter, it doth make:
Never idle, never still,
What a worker is the mill!

Hearken what the rill doth say
As it journeys every day;
Sweet as skylark on the wing,
"Ripple, dipple," it doth sing:
Never idle, never still,
What a worker is the rill!

Listen to the honey-bee
As he dances merrily
To the little fairy's drum
Humming, drumming, drumming, drum:
Never idle, never still,
Humming, drumming, hum he will.

Like the mill, the rill, the bee,
Idleness is not for me.
What says Cock-a-doodle-doo?
"Up, there's work enough for you."
If I work, then, with a will,
It will be but playing still.

E. CAPERN.

* 70 *

THE VOICE OF SPRING.

I AM coming, I am coming!
Hark! the little bee is humming;
See, the lark is soaring high
In the blue and sunny sky;
And the gnats are on the wing,
Wheeling round in airy ring.

See, the yellow catkins[1] cover
All the slender willows over !
And on banks of mossy green
Star-like primroses are seen;
And, their[2] clustering leaves below,
White and purple violets blow.

Hark! the new-born lambs are bleating,
And the cawing rooks[3] are meeting
In the elms, — a noisy crowd;
All the birds are singing loud;
And the first white butterfly
In the sunshine dances by.

Look around thee, look around!
Flowers in all the fields abound;
Every running stream is bright;
All the orchard trees are white;

---

[1] *catkins*, blossoms, — a kind of flower, long and slender, resembling a cat's tail, as in the willows, the hazel, etc.
[2] *their*, that is, the violets' leaves.   [3] *rook*, a bird like a crow.

And each small and waving shoot
Promises sweet flowers and fruit.

Turn thine eyes to earth and heaven:
God for thee the spring has given,
Taught the birds their melodies,[1]
Clothed the earth, and cleared the skies,
For thy pleasure or thy food:
Pour thy soul in gratitude.[2]

- MARY HOWITT.

* 71 *

MAY.

WELCOME, welcome, lovely May!
Breath so sweet, and smiles so gay;
Sun, and dew, and gentle showers,
Welcome, welcome, month of flowers!

Welcome, violets, sweet and blue,
Drinking-cups of morning dew!
Welcome, lambs, so full of glee!
Welcome, too, my busy bee!

Birdies sing on every spray,
Welcome, sunshine! welcome May!
Many a pretty flower uncloses,
And the garden smells of roses.

T. D. MILLER.

---

[1] *melodies*, songs.   [2] be very thankful.

* 72 *

THE SUMMER'S DAY.

FLOWERS are springing,
Birds are singing,
Bees are humming all around;
Joy and pleasure,
Without measure,
Welcome us in every sound.

In the meadows
Lights and shadows
Chase each other far away;
Lambs are bleating,
Swallows fleeting:
Happy all this summer's day.

MATTHIAS BARR.

* 73 *

THE LILY.

COME, my Love, and do not spurn
From a little flower to learn.
See the lily on the bed
Hanging down its modest head,
While it scarcely can be seen,
Folded on its leaf of green.

Yet we love the lily well
For its sweet and pleasant smell,

And would rather call it ours
Than the many gayer flowers:
Pretty lilies seem to be
Emblems[1] of humilty.[2]

Come, my Love, and do not spurn
From a little flower to learn:
Let your temper be as sweet
As the lily at your feet;
Be as gentle, be as mild,
Be a modest, simple child.

'Tis not beauty that we prize;
Like a summer flower it dies;
But humility will last,
Fair and sweet when beauty's past;
And the Saviour from above
Views a humble child with love.

JANE TAYLOR.

* 74 *

THE DAISY.

I'M a pretty little thing,
Always coming with the spring;
In the meadows green I'm found,
Peeping just above the ground;
And my stalk is covered flat
With a white and yellow hat.

---

[1] *emblem*, a sign or symbol.   [2] *humility*, humbleness.

Little lady, when you pass
Lightly o'er the tender grass,
Skip about, but do not tread
On`my meek and lowly head;
For I always seem to say,
Surely winter's gone away.

* 75 *

THE FLY.

WHAT a sharp little fellow is Mr. Fly!
He goes where he pleases, low or high,
And can walk just as well with his feet to the sky
    As I can on the floor.
      At the window he comes
      With a buzz and a roar,
      And o'er the smooth glass
      With ease he can pass,
    Or through the keyhole of the door.
He eats the sugar, and goes away,
Nor ever once asks how much is to pay;
And sometimes he crosses the teapot's steam,
And comes and plunges his head in the cream.

Then on the edge of the jug he stands,
And cleans his wings with his feet and hands;
This done, through the window he hurries away,
And gives a buzz, as if to say,
" At present I haven't a minute to stay;
But I'll peep in again in the course of the day."

Do you know how low and sweet,
O'er the pebbles at their feet,
Are the words the waves repeat
    Night and day?

Have you heard the robins singing,
    Little one,
When the rosy dawn is breaking, —
    When 'tis done?
Have you heard the wooing [1] breeze,
In the blossomed orchard trees,
And the drowsy hum of bees
    In the sun?

All the earth is full of music,
    Little May, —
Bird and bee, and water singing
    On its way.
Let their silver voices fall
On thy heart with happy call:
" Praise the Lord, who loveth all,
    Night and day."
              EMILY HUNTINGTON MILLER.

* 79 *

MERRY ARE THE BELLS.

MERRY are the bells,
  And merry would they ring;
Merry are we all,
    And merry will we sing:

---

[1] *wooing*, gentle, soothing.

With a merry ding-dong,
    Happy, gay, and free,
And a merry sing-song,
    Happy let us be.

Merry have we met,
    And merry have we been;
Merry let us part,
    And merry meet again:
With our merry sing-song,
    Happy, gay, and free,
And a merry ding-dong,
    Happy let us be.

* 80 *

THE LITTLE WORKER'S SONG.

COLD the winter wind is blowing,
And it never ceases snowing, —
Snowing, blowing, all day long;
Yet I sing a merry song.

I like to see the bright fire burning;
I like to know my bread I'm earning;
I like to work, and then to play:
I'm happy, happy, all the day.

Soon will come the spring's soft showers,
And after that the summer flowers;
This makes me happy all day long;
This makes me sing a merry song.

* 81 *

A SWINGING SONG.

MERRY it is on a summer's day
All through the meadows to wend[1] away;
To watch the brooks glide fast or slow,
And the little fish twinkle down below; ·
To hear the birds in the blue sky sing:
Oh! sure enough, 'tis a merry thing;
But 'tis merrier far to swing, to swing.

Merry it is on a winter's night
To listen to tales of elf and sprite,[2]
Of caves and castles[3] so dim and old, —
The dismalest tales that ever were told, —
And then to laugh, and then to sing,
You may take my word, is a merry thing;
But 'tis merrier far to swing, to swing.

Down with the hoop upon the green!
Down with the ringing tambourine![4]
Little heed we for this or for that;
Off with the bonnet, off with the hat!
Away we go like birds on the wing;
Higher yet, higher yet, now for the King![5]
This is the way we swing, we swing.

Scarcely the bough bends, Claude is so light;
Mount up behind him, — there, that is right! —

[1] *wend*, go.   [2] *sprite*, a spirit.
[3] *castle*, a strong building where a prince or a nobleman dwells.
[4] *tambourine*, a kind of shallow drum with one skin, and bells fastened to
the rim.
[5] *King*, the highest swing of all.

Down bends the branch now; swing him away,
Higher yet, higher yet, higher, I say!
Oh, what a joy it is!   Now, let us sing,
"A pear for the Queen, an apple for the King,"
And shake the old tree as we swing, we swing.

* 82 *

THE FAIRY QUEEN'S SONG.

COME follow, follow me,
Ye fairy elves [1] that be; [2]
Light tripping o'er the green,
Come follow Mab, your Queen:
Hand in hand we'll dance around,
For this place is fairy ground.

When mortals are at rest,
And snoring in their nest,
Unheard and unespied,
Through keyholes we do glide;
Over tables, stools, and shelves,
We trip it with our fairy elves.

Upon a mushroom's head
Our table-cloth we spread;
A grain of rye or wheat
The viands [3] that we eat;
Pearly drops of dew we drink
In acorn cups filled to the brink.

[1] *fairy elf* (plural, *elves*), an imaginary or 'make-believe' little being formerly believed to haunt woods and wild places.
[2] that may be or are.   [3] *viands*, food.

And stand amid the drifted snow,
  Like thee, a thing apart,
Than be a man who walks with men,
  But has a frozen heart.

ANNIE D. GREEN.
(MARIAN DOUGLAS.)

* 86 *

DEEDS OF KINDNESS.

SUPPOSE the little cowslip
  Should hang its golden cup,
And say, " I'm such a tiny flower,
  I'd better not grow up."
How many a weary traveller
  Would miss its fragrant smell!
How many a little child would grieve
  To lose it from the dell!

Suppose the glistening dewdrop
  Upon the grass should say,
" What can a little dewdrop do?
  I'd better roll away."
The blade on which it rested,
  Before the day was done,
Without a drop to moisten it,
  Would wither in the sun.

'Suppose the little breezes,
  Upon a summer's day,
Should think themselves too small to cool
  The traveller on his way:

Who would not miss the smallest
    And softest ones that blow,
And think they made a great mistake,
    If they were talking so?

How many deeds of kindness
    A little child may do,
Although it has so little strength,
    And little wisdom too!
It wants a loving spirit,
    Much more than strength, to prove
How many things a child may do
    For others by its love.

F. P.

* 87 *

CHICK-A-DE-DEE.

THE ground was all covered with snow one day,
And two little sisters were busy at play,
When a snow-bird was sitting close by on a tree,
And merrily singing his chick-a-de-dee.
Chick-a-de-dee, chick-a-de-dee!
And merrily singing his chick-a-de-dee.

He had not been singing that tune very long,
Ere Emily heard him, so sweet was his song;
" O sister, look out of the window!" said she:
" Here's a dear little bird singing chick-a-de-dee,
Chick-a-de-dee, chick-a-de-dee;
Here's a dear little bird singing chick-a-de-dee.

" O mother ! do get him some stockings and shoes,
And a nice little frock, and a hat, if you choose ;
I wish he'd come into the parlor, and see
How warm we would make him, poor chick-a-de-dee!
Chick-a-de-dee, chick-a-de-dee !
How warm we would make him, poor chick-a-de-
dee ! "

" There is One, my dear child, though I cannot
tell who,
Has clothed me already, and warm enough, too :
Good-morning !   Oh, who are so happy as we ? "
And away he went, singing his chick-a-de-dee.
Chick-a-de-dee, chick-a-de-dee !
And away he went, singing his chick-a-de-dee.

F. C. Woodworth.

* 88 *

DON'T KILL THE BIRDS.

Don't kill the birds ! — the little birds
    That sing about your door
Soon as the joyous spring has come,
    And chilling storms are o'er.
The little birds, how sweet they sing !
    Oh, let them joyous live !
And never seek to take the life
    That you can never give.

Don't kill the birds ! — the pretty birds
    That play among the trees :

'Twould make the earth a cheerless place,
    Should we dispense with [1] these.
The little birds, how fond they play!
    Do not disturb their sport,
But let them warble forth their songs
    Till winter cuts them short.

Don't kill the birds! — the happy birds
    That bless the field and grove;
So innocent to look upon,
    They claim our warmest love.
The happy birds, the tuneful birds,
    How pleasant 'tis to see!
No spot can be a cheerless place
    Where'er their presence be.

D. C. COLESWORTHY.

* 89 *

GOD'S GOODNESS.

WHO has counted the leaves that fall
    In the autumn from the trees?
Who has counted the grains of sand
    That are hid beneath the seas?

Who has counted how many flowers
    In the fields and gardens grow?
Who, on a gloomy winter's day,
    Has counted the flakes of snow?

---

[1] *dispense with*, do without.

Who has fathomed [1] the deep, deep sea,
  Or numbered the stars at night?
Who has counted the drops of rain,
  Or the rays of sunny light?

None, none but God. He made them all,
  And he knows them every one, —
The stars and flowers, the sands and trees,
  And the bright rays of the sun.

The sea is deep, and reaches far,
  And bright is the sun above:
God's goodness reaches farther still,
  And more brightly shines his love.

* 90 *

VIOLETS.

UNDER the green hedges, after the snow,
There do the dear little violets grow,
Hiding their modest and beautiful heads
Under the hawthorn in soft mossy beds.

Sweet as the roses, and blue as the sky,
Down there do the dear little violets lie,
Hiding their heads where they scarce may be seen;
By the leaves you may know where the violet hath
    been.

M. MOULTRIE.

---

[1] *fathomed*, found out the depth of.

* 91 *

GOD SEES ME.

THROUGH all the busy daylight, through all the
 quiet night,
Whether the stars are in the sky, or the sun is
 shining bright,
In the nursery, in the parlor, in the street, or on
 the stair,
Though I may seem to be alone, yet God is always
 there.
    Whatever I may do,
    Wherever I may be,
    Although I see him not,
    Yet God sees me.

He knows each word I mean to speak, before the
 word is spoken ;
He knows the thoughts within my heart, although
 I give no token.[1]
When I am naughty, then I grieve my Heavenly
 Father's love ;
And, every time I really try, he helps me from
 above.
    Whatever I may do,
    Wherever I may be,
    Although I see him not,
    Yet God sees me.

[1] *token,* sign, that which serves to point out or show any thing.

* 92 *

THE TRUTHFUL PART.

O FATHER, bless a little child,
    And in her early youth
Give her a spirit good and mild,
    A soul to love the truth.

May never falsehood in her heart,
    Nor in her words, abide;[1]
But may she act the truthful part,
    Whatever may betide.[2]

* 93 * .

FLOWERS ARE BLOOMING.

THE flowers are blooming everywhere,
    On every hill and dell;
And, oh, how beautiful they are!
    How fragrant, too, they smell!

The little birds, they spring along,
    And look so glad and gay;
I love to hear their pleasant song,
    I feel as glad as they.

The young lambs bleat and frisk about;
    The bees hum round their hive;
The butterflies are coming out;
    'Tis good to be alive.

[1] *abide*, stay, be present.   [2] *betide*, happen.

* 94 *

THE PET LAMB.

Storm upon the mountain,
  Night upon his throne,
And the little snow-white lamb
  Left alone, alone!
Storm upon the mountain,
  Rainy torrents beating,
And the little snow-white lamb
  Bleating, ever bleating!

Down the glen [1] the shepherd
  Drives his flock afar;
Through the murky [2] mist and cloud
  Shines no beacon [3] star;
Fast he hurries onward,
  Never hears the moan
Of the pretty snow-white lamb
  Left alone, alone!

At the shepherd's doorway
  Stands his little son,
Sees the sheep come trooping home,
  Counts them one by one,
Counts them full and fairly;
  Trace he findeth none
Of the snow-white lamb
  Left alone, alone!

[1] *glen*, deep narrow valley.   [2] *murky*, black, gloomy.
[3] *beacon*, guiding.

Up the glen he races,
  Breasts [1] the bitter wind,
Scours [2] across the plain, and leaves
  Wood and wold [3] behind.
Storm upon the mountain,
  Night upon his throne;
There he finds the little lamb,
  Left alone, alone!

Struggling, panting, sobbing,
  Kneeling on the ground,
Round the pretty creature's neck
  Both his arms are wound;
Soon, within his bosom,
  All its bleatings done,
Home he bears the little lamb
  Left alone, alone!

Oh the happy faces
  By the shepherd's fire!
High without the tempest roars;
  But the laugh rings higher:
Young and old together
  Make that joy their own;
In their midst the little lamb
  Left alone, alone!

[1] *breasts*, faces, bears the breast against.   [2] *scours*, runs swiftly.
[3] *wold*, a tract of hilly land.

* 95 *

A LITTLE GIRL'S GOOD-BY.

GOOD-BY, daisy, pink, and rose,
    And snow-white lily too!
Every pretty flower that grows:
    Here's a kiss for you.

Good-by, merry bird and bee!
    And take this tiny song
For the one you sang to me
    All the summer long.

Good-by, mossy little rill,
    That shivers in the cold!
Leaves that fall on vale and hill
    Cover you with gold.[1]

A sweet good-by to birds that roam,[2]
    And rills, and flowers and bees;
But when winter's[3] gone, come home
    As early as you please.
                GEORGE COOPER.

* 96 *

THE BIRD'S SONG.

A LITTLE bird with feathers brown
    Sat singing on a tree;
The song was very soft and low,
    But sweet as it could be.

---

[1] gold-colored leaves.   [2] *roam*, go from place to place.
[3] *winter's*, winter is.

And all the people passing by
  Looked up to see the bird
That made the sweetest melody[1]
  That ever they had heard.

But all the bright eyes looked in vain,
  For birdie was so small;
And with a modest dark brown coat
  He made no show at all.

" Papa dear," little Gracie said,
  " Where can this birdie be?
If I could sing a song like that
  I'd sit where folks could see."

" I hope my little girl will learn
  A lesson from that bird,
And try to do what good she can, —
  Not to be seen or heard.

" This birdie is content to sit
  Unnoticed by the way,
And sweetly sing his Maker's praise
  From dawn to close of day.

" So live, my child, all through your life,
  That, be it short or long,
Though others may forget your looks,
  They'll not forget your song."

---

[1] *melody*, music.

And just as many daisies
As their soft hands can hold.

p. 20.

Select Poetry for Young Folks.

* 1 *

THE PIPER.

PIPING [1] down the valleys wild,
　Piping songs of pleasant glee,
On a cloud I saw a child,
　And he, laughing, said to me, —

"Pipe a song about a lamb : "
　So I piped with merry cheer.
"Piper, pipe that song again : "
　So I piped; he wept to hear.

"Drop thy pipe, thy happy pipe,
　Sing thy songs of happy cheer : "
So I sang the same again,
　While he wept with joy to hear.

"Piper, sit thee down and write
　In a book, that all may read : "
So he vanished from my sight.
　And I plucked a hollow reed,[2]

[1] *piping*, playing on a musical pipe, — a kind of flute.
[2] *reed*, a plant or grass having a hollow jointed stem.

3

And I made a rural[1] pen,
    And I stained[2] the water clear,
And I wrote my happy songs,
    Every child may joy to hear.

W. BLAKE

* 2 *

ANSWER TO A CHILD'S QUESTION.

Do you ask what the birds say? The sparrow,
    the dove,
The linnet, and thrush say, "I love and I love!"
In the winter they're silent, the wind is so strong;
What it says I don't know, but it sings a loud
    song.
But green leaves and blossoms, and sunny warm
    weather,
And singing and loving, all come back together;
Then the lark is so brimful of gladness and love,
The green fields below him, the blue sky above,
That he sings, and he sings, and forever sings he,
"I love my Love, and my Love loves me."

S. T. COLERIDGE.

* 3 *

THE BLUEBIRD.

I KNOW the song that the bluebird is singing,
Out in the apple-tree where he is swinging.
Brave little fellow! the skies may be dreary,
Nothing cares he while his heart is so cheery.

---

[1] *rural*, simple, rude.   [2] *stained*, colored or made inky.

Hark! how the music leaps out from his throat!
Hark! was there ever so merry a note?
Listen awhile, and you'll hear what he's saying,
Up in the apple-tree, swinging and swaying:

" Dear little blossoms, down under the snow,
You must be weary of winter, I know;
Hark! while I sing you a message of cheer,
Summer is coming, and spring-time is here!

" Little white snowdrop, I pray you arise;
Bright yellow crocus, come, open your eyes
Sweet little violets hid from the cold,
Put on your mantles of purple and gold;
Daffodils, daffodils! say, do you hear?
Summer is coming, and spring-time is here!"
                                    EMILY HUNTINGTON MILLER.

* 4 *

THE DAISY.

BEFORE the stars are in the sky,
    The daisy goes to rest,
And folds its little shining leaves
    Upon its golden breast.

And so it sleeps in dewy night
    Until the morning breaks,
Then, with the songs of early birds,
    So joyously awakes.

And children, when they go to bed,
    Should fold their hands in prayer,
And place themselves and all they love
    In God's protecting care.

Then they may sleep secure and still
    Through hours of darksome[1] night,
And with the pretty daisy wake
    In cheerful morning light.

* 5 *

WINTER JEWELS.

A MILLION little diamonds
    Twinkled on the trees;
And all the little maidens said,
    "A jewel, if you please!"

But, while they held their hands outstretched
    To catch the diamonds gay,
A million little sunbeams came
    And stole them all away.

* 6 *

LADY-BIRD, LADY-BIRD.

LADY-BIRD,[2] lady-bird, fly away home!
    The field-mouse is gone to her nest;

---

[1] *darksome*, dark, gloomy.   [2] *lady-bird*, a small spotted beetle.

The daisies have shut up their little bright eyes,
   And the bees and the birds are at rest.

Lady-bird, lady-bird, fly away home!
   The glowworm is lighting her lamp;
The dew's falling fast, and your fine speckled
     wings
   Will be wet with the close-clinging damp.

Lady-bird, lady-bird, fly away home!
   The fairy bells tinkle afar;
Make haste, or they'll catch you, and harness you
     fast,
   With a cobweb, to Oberon's [1] car.

CAROLINE BOWLES SOUTHEY.

* 7 *

A LAUGHING SONG.

WHEN the green woods laugh with the voice of
     joy,
And the dimpling stream runs laughing by;
When the air does laugh with our merry wit,
And the green hill laughs with the noise of it;

When the meadows laugh with lively green,
And the grasshopper laughs in the merry scene;
When Mary, and Susan, and Emily,
With their sweet round mouths, sing "Ha, ha,
     he!"

---

[1] *Ob'eron*, the imaginary king of the fairies.

When the painted birds laugh in the shade
Where our table with cherries and nuts is
　　spread, —
Come live, and be merry, and join with me
To sing the sweet chorus of " Ha, ha, he!"

W. BLAKE.

* 8 *

A BOAT SONG.

THE morn shines bright,
And the bark bounds light
　　As the stag bounds o'er the lea:[1]
We love the strife
Of the sailor's life,
　　And we love our dark-blue sea.

Now high, now low,
To the depths we go,
　　Now rise to the surge again:
We make a track
On the Ocean's back,
　　And play with his hoary mane.[2]

Fearless we face
The storm in its chase,
　　When the dark clouds fly before it,
And meet the shock
Of the fierce Siroc,[3]
　　Though death breathes hotly o'er it.

---

[1] *lea*, grass-land.　　　[2] *hoary mane*, white tops of the waves.
[3] *Siroc*, the Sirocco, a hot wind from the Great Desert of Africa.

The landsman may quail
At the shout of the gale,
　　Which peril's[1] the sailor's joy;
But wild as the waves
Which his vessel braves,
　　Is the lot of the sailor boy.
Sir E. B. Lytton.

* 9 *

THE FAIRIES.

Up the airy[2] mountain,
　　Down the rushy[3] glen,
We daren't go a-hunting
　　For fear of little men;
Wee[4] folk, good folk,
　　Trooping all together, —
Green jacket, red cap,
　　And white owl's feather!

Down along the rocky shore
　　Some make their home;
They live on crispy pancakes
　　Of yellow tide-foam;
Some in the reeds
　　Of the black mountain lake,
With frogs for their watch-dogs,
　　All night awake.

---

[1] *peril's*, peril is.　　　　　　[2] *airy*, high in air.
[3] *rushy*, containing rushes, plants with round stems and no leaves.
　　　　　　　[4] *wee*, little.

High on the hill-top
　　The old King sits;
He is now so old and gray
　　He's nigh lost his wits.

With a bridge of white mist
　　Columbkill[1] he crosses
On his stately journeys
　　From Slieveleague[1] to Rosses;[1]
Or going up with music
　　On cold starry nights,
To sup with the Queen
　　Of the gay Northern Lights.[2]

They stole little Bridget,
　　For seven years long;
When she came down again,
　　Her friends were all gone.
They took her lightly back,
　　Between the night and morrow;
They thought that she was fast asleep;
　　But she was dead with sorrow.

They have kept her ever since
　　Deep within the lakes,
On a bed of flag-leaves,
　　Watching till she wakes.

---

[1] *Columbkill*, a glen between *Slieveleague*, a mountain, and *Rosses*, islands
on the coast of Donegal, Ireland.

[2] *Northern Lights*, the bright streamers sometimes seen in the northern
sky, — called, also, *aurora borealis*.

By the craggy hillside,
   Through the mosses bare,
They have planted thorn-trees
   For pleasure here and there.
Is any man so daring
   As dig one up in spite,
He shall find the thornies [1] set
   In his bed at night.

Up the airy mountain,
   Down the rushy glen,
We daren't go a-hunting,
   For fear of little men;
Wee folk, good folk,
   Trooping all together, —
Green jacket, red cap,
   And white owl's feather!

W. ALLINGHAM.

* 10 *

THE BROWN THRUSH.

THERE's a merry brown thrush sitting up in the
   tree:
He's singing to me; he's singing to me!
And what does he say, little girl, little boy?
 "Oh, the world's running over with joy!
   Don't you hear? Don't you see?
   Hush! Look! In my tree
I'm as happy as happy can be!"

---

[1] *thornies*, thorns, prickles.

And the brown thrush keeps singing, "A nest, do
    you see,
And five eggs hid by me in the juniper-tree?[1]
Don't meddle, don't touch! little girl, little boy,
  Or the world will lose some of its joy:
     Now I'm glad! now I'm free!
     And I always shall be,
If you never bring sorrow to me."

So the merry brown thrush sings away in the tree,
  To you and to me, to you and to me;
And he sings all the day, little girl, little boy:
  "Oh, the world's running over with joy!
     But long it won't be —
     Don't you know? don't you see? —
  Unless we are as good as can be!"

                         LUCY LARCOM.

✴ 11 ✴

ROBERT OF LINCOLN.

MERRILY swinging on brier and weed,
  Near to the nest of his little dame,
Over the mountain-side or mead,
  Robert of Lincoln is telling his name:
    Bob-o'-link, bob-o'-link,
    Spink, spank, spink;
Snug and safe is that nest of ours,
Hidden among the summer flowers.
    Chee, chee, chee.

---

[1] *Juniper-tree,* a kind of evergreen tree.

Robert of Lincoln is gayly dressed,
   Wearing a bright black wedding-coat;
White are his shoulders, and white his crest;
   Hear him call in his merry note:
     Bob-o'-link, bob-o'-link,
     Spink, spank, spink;
Look what a nice new coat is mine,
Sure there was never a bird so fine.
     Chee, chee, chee.

Robert of Lincoln's Quaker wife,
   Pretty and quiet, with plain brown wings,
Passing at home a patient life,
   Broods[1] in the grass while her husband sings:
     Bob-o'-link, bob-o'-link,
     Spink, spank, spink;
Brood, kind creature: you need not fear
Thieves and robbers while I am here.
     Chee, chee, chee.

Modest and shy as a nun is she;
   One weak chirp is her only note;
Braggart, and prince of braggarts, is he,
   Pouring boasts from his little throat:
     Bob-o'-link, bob-o'-link,
     Spink, spank, spink;
Never was I afraid of man;
Catch me, cowardly knaves,[2] if you can!
     Chee, chee, chee.

---

[1] *broods*, sits on her eggs to hatch them.   [2] *knaves*, bad fellows.

Six white eggs on a bed of hay,
    Flecked [1] with purple, a pretty sight!
There as the mother sits all day,
    Robert is singing with all his might:
      Bob-o'-link, bob-o'-link,
      Spink, spank, spink;
Nice good wife that never goes out,
Keeping house while I frolic about.
      Chee, chee, chee.

Soon as the little ones chip the shell,
    Six wide mouths are open for food;
Robert of Lincoln bestirs him well,
    Gathering seeds for the hungry brood.
      Bob-o'-link, bob-o'-link,
      Spink, spank, spink;
This new life is likely to be
Hard for a gay young fellow like me.
      Chee, chee, chee.

Robert of Lincoln at length is made
    Sober with work and silent with care;
Off is his holiday garment laid,
    Half forgotten that merry air:
      Bob-o'-link, bob-o'-link,
      Spink, spank, spink;
Nobody knows but my mate and I
Where our nest and our nestlings lie:
      Chee, chee, chee,

---

[1] *flecked*, streaked or spotted.

Summer wanes;[1] the children are grown;
Fun and frolic no more he knows;
Robert of Lincoln's[2] a humdrum crone;[3]
Off he flies, and we sing as he goes,
Bob-o'-link, bob-o'-link,
Spink, spank, spink;
When you can pipe that merry old strain,
Robert of Lincoln, come back again.
Chee, chee, chee.
WILLIAM CULLEN BRYANT.

* 12 *

ROBIN REDBREAST.

GOOD-BY, good-by to Summer!
For Summer's nearly done;
The garden smiling faintly,
Cool breezes in the sun.
Our thrushes now are silent,
Our swallows flown away;
But Robin's here, with coat of brown,
And ruddy breast-knot gay.

Robin, Robin Redbreast,
O Robin dear!
Robin sings so sweetly
In the falling of the year!

---

[1] *wanes*, is near its end.   [2] *Lincoln's*, Lincoln is.
[3] *crone*, an old woman.

Bright yellow, red, and orange,
  The leaves come down in hosts;
The trees are Indian princes,
  But soon they'll turn to ghosts;
The scanty pears and apples
  Hang russet on the bough:
It's Autumn, Autumn, Autumn late,
  'Twill soon be Winter now.

    Robin, Robin Redbreast,
      O Robin dear!
    And what will this poor Robin do?
      For pinching days are near.

The fireside for the cricket,
  The wheat-stack for the mouse,
When trembling night-winds whistle
  And moan all round the house.
The frosty twigs like iron,
  The branches plumed with snow, —
Alas! in Winter dead and dark,
  Where can poor Robin go?

    Robin, Robin Redbreast,
      O Robin dear!
    And a crumb of bread for Robin,
      His little heart to cheer!

               W. ALLINGHAM.

* 13 *

THE BROOK.

WHERE are you running so fast, little brook,
  Over the stones so gray?
Stop for a moment, I prithee,[1] dear brook, —
  Just for a moment, and play.

You chatter away as you flow, little brook,
  But speak to me never a word,
Though often I whisper to you, little brook,
  Sweet secrets by others unheard.

Oh! what do you say to the birds, little brook,
  That fly to your bosom to drink?
Oh! what do you say to the flowers, dear brook,
  That cluster so close to your brink?

And what do you say to yourself, little brook,
  As you ripple in music along?
The while that I fill my pitcher, dear brook,
  Please tell me the words of your song.

You are hasting away to the sea, dear brook,
  To the great, unfathoméd[2] sea;
You may not delay for a moment, dear brook:
  Is that what you whisper to me?

---

[1] *I prithee* (*th* sounded as in *this*), I pray thee.
[2] *unfathoméd*, not sounded to find out the depth.

Ah! then, is your life like ours, little brook,
   Ever hurrying, hurrying on,
Till the waves of an unknown sea, little brook,
   We reach some day, and are gone.

Mrs. Charles Heaton.

* 14 *

CHERISH KINDLY FEELINGS.

Cherish kindly feelings, children,
   Nurse them in your heart;
Don't forget to take them with you
   When from home you start.
In the schoolroom, in the parlor,
   At your work or play,
Kindly thoughts and kindly feelings
   Cherish every day.

Cherish kindly feelings, children,
   While on earth you stay.
They will scatter light and sunshine
   All along your way,
Make the path of duty brighter,
   Make your trials less,
And, whate'er your lot or station,
   Bring you happiness.

M. A. Kidder.

* 15 *

FAULTS OF OTHERS.

WHAT are another's faults to me?
    I've not a vulture's bill
To pick at every flaw I see,
    And make it wider still.

It is enough for me to know
    I've follies of my own,
And on my heart the care bestow,
    And let my friends alone.
                D. C. COLESWORTHY.

* 16 *

MARCH.

THE cock is crowing,
The stream is flowing,
The small birds twitter,
The lake doth glitter,
The green field sleeps in the sun:
    The oldest and youngest
    Are at work with the strongest;
    The cattle are grazing,
    Their heads never raising;
There are forty feeding like one!

    Like an army defeated
    The snow hath retreated,

And now doth fare ill[1]
On the top of the bare hill;
The plough-boy is whooping anon, anon;[2]
There's joy in the mountains;
There's life in the fountains;
Small clouds are sailing,
Blue sky prevailing;[3]
The rain is over and gone!

W. WORDSWORTH.

* 17 *

SPRING.

THE alder by the river
Shakes out her powdery curls;
The willow buds[4] in silver
For little boys and girls.

The little birds fly over,
And oh, how sweet they sing!
To tell the happy children
That once again 'tis spring.

The gay green grass comes creeping
So soft beneath their feet;
The frogs begin to ripple
A music clear and sweet.

[1] gets on badly (as it is melting away).   [3] *prevailing*, becoming general.
[2] *anon*, at times.   [4] *buds*, puts forth buds.

And buttercups are coming,
  And scarlet columbine;
And in the sunny meadows
  The dandelions shine.

And just as many daisies
  As their soft hands can hold
The little ones may gather,
  All fair in white and gold.

Here blows the warm red clover,
  There peeps the violet blue;
O happy little children,
  God made them all for you!
                            CELIA THAXTER.

* 18 *

BIRDS IN SUMMER.

How pleasant the life of a bird must be,
Flitting about in each leafy tree! —
In the leafy trees so broad and tall,
Like a green and beautiful palace hall,
With its airy chambers, light and boon,[1]
That open to sun and stars and moon;
That open unto the bright blue sky,
And the frolicsome winds as they wander by!

They have left their nests on the forest bough —
Those homes of delight they need not now;

---

[1] *boon,* gay, cheerful.

And the young and the old they wander out,
And traverse [1] their green world round about;
And hark! at the top of this leafy hall,
How one to the other in love they call!
"Come up, come up!" they seem to say,
"Where the topmost twigs in the breezes sway.

"Come up, come up! for the world is fair
Where the merry leaves dance in the summer air."
And the birds below give back the cry:
"We come, we come, to the branches high.".
How pleasant the life of a bird must be,
Flitting about in a leafy tree!
And away through the air what joy to go,
And to look on the bright green earth below!

MARY HOWITT.

* 19 *

HIE AWAY.

HIE [2] away, hie away!
Over bank and over brae, [3] .
Where the copsewood [4] is the greenest,
Where the fountains glisten sheenest, [5]
Where the lady-fern grows strongest,
Where the morning dew lies longest,
Where the blackcock sweetest sips it,
Where the fairy latest trips it: [6]

---

[1] *traverse*, pass over or through.   [2] *hie*, hasten.
[3] *brae* (pronounced 'bray'), a Scottish word meaning 'a slope of a hill.'
[4] *copsewood*, wood of small growth.   [5] *sheenest*, brightest.
[6] *trips it*, runs or steps lightly or nimbly.

Hie to haunts right seldom seen,
Lovely, lonesome, cool, and green,
Over bank and over brae,
Hie away, hie away!

SIR WALTER SCOTT.

* 20 *

WINTER.

OLD Winter is a sturdy one,
And lasting stuff he's made of;
His flesh is firm as iron-stone;
There's nothing he's afraid of.

He spreads his coat upon the heath,[1]
Nor yet to warm it lingers;
He scouts[2] the thought of aching teeth,
Or chilblains on his fingers.

Of flowers that bloom, or birds that sing,
Full little cares or knows he;
He hates the fire, and hates the Spring,
And all that's warm and cosey.

But when the foxes bark aloud
On frozen hill and river,
When round the fire the people crowd,
And rub their hands, and shiver,

[1] *heath*, an open waste tract of land.
[2] *scouts*, sneers or laughs at.

When frost is splitting stone and wall,
    And trees come crashing after, —
That hates he not, he loves it all, —
    Then bursts he out in laughter.

His home is by the North Pole's strand,[1]
    Where earth and sea are frozen;
His summer-house, we understand,
    In Switzerland he's chosen.

Now from the North he's hither hied
    To show his strength and power;
And, when he comes, we stand aside,
    And look at him, and cower.[2]

FROM THE GERMAN.

* 21 *

HARVEST-HOME.

HARK! from woodlands far away
    Sounds the merry roundelay;[3]
Now, across the russet[4] plain,
    Slowly moves the loaded wain;[5]
Greet the reapers as they come —
Happy, happy harvest-home![6]

Never fear the wintry blast,
    Summer suns will shine at last;

---

[1] *strand*, shore, beach of the sea.   [2] *cower*, shrink, or crouch.
roundelay, a song in which the passages or parts are repeated.
russet, reddish-brown.   [5] *wain*, wagon.
[6] *harvest-home*, time of bringing home the harvest.

See the golden grain appear,
See the produce of the year.
Greet the reapers as they come —
Happy, happy harvest-home!

Children join the jocund [1] ring,
Young and old come forth and sing;
Stripling blithe,[2] and maiden gay,
Hail the rural holiday.
Greet the reapers as they come —
Happy, happy harvest-home!

Peace and plenty be our lot,
All the pangs of war forgot; .
Strength to toil, and ample store,
Bless our country evermore!
Greet the reapers as they come—
Happy, happy harvest-home!

* 22 *

THE FOUR SEASONS.

SPRING.

SPRING day, happy day!
God hath made the earth so gay!
Every little flower he waketh;
Every herb to grow he maketh.
When the pretty lambs are springing,
When the little birds are singing,
Child, forget not God to praise,
Who hath sent such happy days.

---

[1] *jocund*, merry,   [2] *blithe* (pron. ' blīth,' — *th* as in ' *this* '), joyful.

SUMMER.

Summer day, sultry day !
Hotly burns the noontide [1] ray ;
Gentle drops of summer showers
Fall on thirsty trees and flowers ;
On the cornfield [2] rain doth pour,
Ripening grain for winter store.
Child, to God thy thanks should be,
Who in summer thinks of thee.

AUTUMN.

Autumn day, fruitful day !
See what God hath given away !
Orchard trees with fruit are bending ;
Harvest wains [3] are homeward wending ; [4]
And the Lord all o'er the land
Opens wide his bounteous hand.
Children, gathering fruits that fall,
Think of God, who gives them all.

WINTER.

Winter day, frosty day !
God a cloak on all doth lay ;
On the earth the snow he sheddeth ;
O'er the lamb a fleece he spreadeth ;
Gives the bird a coat of feather
To protect it from the weather ;
Gives the children home and food.
Let us praise him : God is good.

---

[1] *noontide*, noon-time, mid-day.　　　[3] *wains*, wagons.
[2] *cornfield*, field of wheat or other grain.　　[4] *wending*, going.

She loved them as only a mother loves,
  And sang them her songs of glee :
There were no little birds more happy than they,
  In their home in the chosen tree.

Put one of this little family
  Grew tired of his mother's care;
He sat all day in a sullen mood,
  And nought to him was fair.

For the heart of this little bird was changed,
  And he thought he should like to roam
Away o'er the fields and the high green hills,
  In search of a brighter home.

II.

Ah me ! there is not a brighter home
  Than that which is lighted by love ;
There is no other light so divinely sweet, —
  Not the moon nor the stars above.

But he fled away, and he sported awhile
  Amid flowers of rich perfume and hue ;
But when night came on, he was weary and cold,
  And it rained, and the storm-wind blew.

Ah ! then he thought of his mother's wing,
  Which had covered him tenderly,
And his little brothers, so happy and good,
  In their home in the chosen tree.

Then he lifted his voice; but none to hear
　The sound of his sorrow were nigh;
So he covered his head with his half-fledged wing
　And he sat on a stone to die.

Oh! never more in that beautiful wood
　Was the sound of his gladness heard;
And for many a day did his brothers weep
　For the loss of the truant bird.

And for many a day no song of joy
　Came up from his mother's breast:
She mourned for him with drooping wings;
　But he came not again to his nest.

And thus, little children, from this you may learn
　How even one child may be
The cause of sorrow, which nought may remove,
　From a little family.

You each have a home in a chosen tree,
　Which your parents have lighted with love:
Oh! cause not the shadows of grief to descend,
　The beautiful light to remove.

looked on the peasant's lowly cot, —
omething of sadness had wrapt the spot,
ut a gleam of *thee* on its lattice fell,
nd it laughed into beauty at that bright
spell.

unbeam of Summer! Oh, what is like thee,
[ope of the wilderness, joy of the sea!
- *One* thing is like thee to mortals given,
he faith touching all things with hues of heaven!

FELICIA HEMANS.

* 33 *

WE ARE SEVEN.

I.

I MET a little cottage girl:
  She was eight years old, she said;
Her hair was thick with many a curl
  That clustered round her head.

She had a rustic, woodland air,
  And she was wildly clad:
Her eyes were fair, and very fair;
  Her beauty made me glad.

" Sisters and brothers, little Maid,
  How many may you be? "
" How many? Seven in all," she said,
  And wondering looked at me.

" And where are they?   I pray you tell."
   She answered, " Seven are we ;
And two of us at Conway dwell,
   And two are gone to sea;

" Two of us in the churchyard lie, —
   My sister and my brother ;
And in the churchyard cottage I
   Dwell near them with my mother."

" You say that two at Conway dwell,
   And two are gone to sea,
Yet ye are seven ! — I pray you tell,
   Sweet Maid, how this may be."

Then did the little Maid reply :
   " Seven boys and girls are we ;
Two of us in the churchyard lie,
   Beneath the churchyard tree."

" You run about, my little Maid,
   Your limbs they are alive ;
If two are in the churchyard laid,
   Then ye are only five."

II.

" Their graves are green, they may be seen,"
   The little Maid replied.
" Twelve steps or more from my mother's do
   And they are side by side.

" My stockings there I often knit,
　My kerchief[1] there I hem;
And there upon the ground I sit, —
　I sit and sing to them.

" And often after sunset, Sir,
　When it is light and fair,
I take my little porringer,[2]
　And eat my supper there.

" The first that died was Sister Jane;
　In bed she moaning lay
Till God released her of her pain,
　And then she went away.

" So in the churchyard she was laid;
　And when the grass was dry,
Together round her grave we played, —
　My brother John and I.

" And when the ground was white with snow,
　And I could run and slide,
My brother John was forced to go,
　And he lies by her side."

" How many are you, then," said I,
　"If they two are in heaven?"
The little Maiden did reply,
　" O master! we are seven."

[1] *kerchief*, a piece of cloth used in dress, especially one for the head.
[2] *porringer*, a small dish for porridge.

" But they are dead; those two are dead:
   Their spirits are in heaven!"
'Twas throwing words away; for still
The little Maid would have her will,
   And said, " Nay, we are seven!"

W. WORDSWORTH.

* 34 *

GOOD-NIGHT AND GOOD-MORNING.

A FAIR little girl sat under a tree
Sewing as long as her eyes could see;
Then smoothed her work, and folded it right,
And said, " Dear work, good-night, good-night!"

Such a number of rooks[1] came over her head,
Crying, " Caw, caw!" on their way to bed;
She said, as she watched their curious flight,
" Little black things, good-night, good-night!"

The horses neighed, and the oxen lowed;
The sheep's " Bleat, bleat!" came over the road,
All seeming to say, with a quiet delight,
" Good little girl, good-night, good-night!"

She did not say to the sun, " Good-night!"
Though she saw him there, like a ball of light;
For she knew he had God's own time to keep
All over the world, and never could sleep.

---

[1] *rook*, a bird like a crow.

* 36 *

LITTLE BELL.

I.

PIPED the blackbird on the woodland spray,[1]
" Pretty maid, slowly wandering this way,
What's your name ? " Quoth he,[2]
" What's your name ?   Oh, stop, and straight un-
fold,[3]
Pretty maid with showery curls of gold."
" Little Bell," said she.

Little Bell sat down beneath the rocks,
Tossed aside her gleaming golden locks,
" Bonny bird ! " quoth she,
" Sing me your best song before I go."
" Here's the very finest song I know,
Little Bell," said he.

And the blackbird piped; you never heard
Half so gay a song from any bird, —
Full of quips and wiles :[4]
Now so round and rich, now soft and slow,
All for love of that sweet face below,
Dimpled o'er with smiles.

And the while[5] the bonny bird did pour
His full heart out freely o'er and o'er
'Neath the morning skies,

[1] *spray*, sprig, twig.
[2] *quoth*, (kwŏth), said.
[3] *straight unfold*, quickly tell.
[4] *quips and wiles*, odd and sly variations.
[5] *the while*, during the time that, while.

In the little childish heart below
All the sweetness seemed to grow and grow,
And shine forth in happy overflow
    From the blue, bright eyes.

Down the dell she tripped; and through the glade
Peeped the squirrel from the hazel shade,
    And from out the tree
Swung and leaped and frolicked, void of fear,
While bold blackbird piped, that all might hear,
'   "Little Bell!" piped he.

II.

Little Bell sat down amid the fern:
"Squirrel, squirrel, to your task return;
    Bring me nuts!" quoth she.
Up, away, the frisky squirrel hies,
Golden wood lights glancing in his eyes;
    And adown the tree,
Great ripe nuts, kissed brown by July sun,
In the little lap drop, one by one:
Hark, how blackbird pipes to see the fun!
    "Happy Bell!" pipes he.

Little Bell looked up and down the glade:
"Squirrel, squirrel, from the nut-tree shade,
Bonny blackbird, if you're not afraid,
    Come and share with me!"
Down came squirrel, eager for his fare,
Down came bonny blackbird, I declare.
Little Bell gave each his honest share,
    Ah the merry three!

And the while those frolic playmates twain [1]
Piped and frisked from bough to bough again,
  'Neath the morning skies,
In the little childish heart below
All the sweetness seemed to grow and grow,
And shine out in happy overflow
  From the blue, bright eyes.

By her snow-white cot, at close of day,
Knelt sweet Bell with folded palms to pray ;
  Very calm and clear
Rose the praying voice to where, unseen
In blue heaven, an angel shape [2] serene
  Paused awhile to hear.

" What good child is this," the angel said,
" That with happy heart beside her bed
  Prays so lovingly ? "
Low and soft, oh, very low and soft,
Crooned [3] the blackbird in the orchard croft,[4]
" Bell, *dear* Bell ! " crooned he.

J. WESTWOOD.

* 37 *

A SHORT SERMON.

CHILDREN who read my lay,[5]
This much I have to say :

---

[1] *twain*, two. [3] *crooned*, hummed, or sang in a low tone.
[2] *shape*, form. [4] *orchard croft*, patch of ground planted with fruit trees.
      [5] *lay*, song, poem.

Each day, and every day,
  Do what is right, —
Right things in great and small,
Then, though the sky should fall,
Sun, moon, and stars, and all,
  You shall have light.

This further would I say:
Be you tempted as you may,
Each day, and every day,
  Speak what is true, —
True things in great and small;
Then, though the sky should fall,
Sun, moon, and stars, and all,
  Heaven would show through.

Figs, as you see and know,
Do not out of thistles grow;
And, though the blossoms blow
  While on the tree,
Grapes never, never yet
On the limbs of thorns were set:
So, if you good would get,[1]
  Good you must be.

Life's journey through and through,
Speaking what is just and true,
Doing what is right to do
  Unto one and all,

[1] get or receive good.

When you work and when you play,
Each day, and every day, —
Then peace shall gild your way,
Though the sky should fall.

ALICE CARY.

* 38 *

WHICH IS YOUR LOT?

SOME children roam the fields and hills,
And others work in noisy mills;
Some dress in silks, and dance and play,
While others drudge their lives away;
Some glow with health, and bound with song,
And some must suffer all day long.

Which is your lot, my girl and boy?
Is it a life of ease and joy?
Ah! if it is, its glowing sun
The poorer life should shine upon.
Make glad one little heart to-day,
And help one burdened child to play.

* 39 *

NEVER PUT OFF.

WHENE'ER a duty waits for thee,
With sober judgment view it,
And never idly wish it done:
Begin at once, and do it.

For Sloth[1] says falsely, " By and by
    Is just as well to do it: "
But present strength is surest strength :
    Begin at once, and do it.

And find not lions in the way,
    Nor faint if thorns bestrew it;[2]
But bravely try, and strength will come,
    For God will help thee to it.

* 40 *

NIGHT.

THE sun descending in the west,
    The evening star does shine ;
The birds are silent in their nest,
    And I must seek for mine.
      The moon, like a flower
      In heaven's high bower,
      With silent delight
    Sits and smiles on the night.

Farewell, green fields and happy groves,
    Where flocks have ta'en[3] delight;
Where lambs have nibbled, silent moves
    The feet of angels bright ;

---

[1] *sloth* (slōth), laziness.   [2] *bestrew it* (be-stroo'), are scattered over it.
[3] *ta'en*, taken.

Unseen, they pour blessing,   •
And joy without ceasing,
On each bud and blossom,
And each sleeping bosom.

They look in every thoughtless nest,
  Where birds are covered warm,
They visit caves of every beast,
  To keep them all from harm : —
If they see any weeping
That should have been sleeping,
They pour sleep on their head,
And sit down by their bed.

W. BLAKE.

* 41 *

WHAT CAN LITTLE HANDS DO?

Oh, what can little hands do
To please the King of heaven ?
The little hands some work may try,
To help the poor in misery.
    Such grace to mine be given !

Oh, what can little lips do
To please the King of heaven ?
The little lips can praise and pray,
And gentle words of kindness say.
    Such grace to mine be given !

Oh, what can little eyes do
To please the King of heaven?
The little eyes can upward look,
Can learn to read God's holy book.
　　Such grace to mine be given!

Oh, what can little hearts do
To please the King of heaven?
The hearts, if God his Spirit send,
Can love and trust the children's Friend.
　　Such grace to mine be given!

Though small is all that we can do
To please the King of heaven,
When hearts and hands and lips unite
To serve the Saviour with delight,
They are most precious in his sight.
　　Such grace to mine be given!

* 42 *

THE MONTHS.

JANUARY, icy cold,
　　Leaves a mantle soft and white;
February, sharp and bold,
　　Onward takes his busy flight.

March's chilly breezes blow,
　　Still they're touched by Winter's hand;
April melts the frozen snow;
　　April sunshine floods the land.

May awakes the sleeping flowers,
  Reigns a sweet and happy queen;
With her coaxing sun and showers
  Robes the trees in tender green.

June is bright with roses gay;
  Harebells bloom around her feet;
Hot July rakes new-mown hay
  From the meadows fresh and sweet.

August's pleasant, quiet reign
  Bids the meadow-lilies come;
And September's golden grain
  Makes a welcome harvest-home.

Glad October's shining sun
  Paints the leaves in richest dyes;
And November, dreary one,
  Shoots his arrows as he flies.

Cold December's latest breath
  Makes the woods and meadows drear,
And his eyelids close in death,
  As he ends the happy year.

DORA READ GOODALE.
(In *"Apple Blossoms."*)

* 43 *

HIGH AND LOW.

THE showers fall as softly
   Upon the lowly grass
As on the stately roses
   That tremble as they pass.

The sunlight shines as brightly
   On fern-leaves bent and torn
As on the golden harvest,
   The fields of waving corn.

The wild birds sing as sweetly
   To rugged, jagged pines,
As to the blossomed orchards,
   And to the cultured vines.

Our Father looks as kindly
   Upon the lowly poor
As on the rich and haughty
   Who turn them from their door.

DORA READ GOODALE.
(In "Apple Blossoms.")

* 44 *

THE WORDS WE SPEAK.

FROM rosy bowers we issue forth,
From east to west, from south to north:
Unseen, unfelt, by night, by day,
Abroad we take our airy way.

We foster love, and kindle strife, —
The bitter and the sweet of life;
Piercing and sharp, we wound like steel;
Now, smooth as oil, those wounds we heal.

Not strings of pearl are valued more,
Nor gems enchased[1] in golden ore;
Yet thousands of us every day,
Worthless and vile, are thrown away.

Ye wise, secure with bars of brass
The double doors through which we pass;
For, once escaped, back to our cell
No human art can us compel.

* 45 *

THE LADY WEAVER.

A LADY weaveth at her loom,
   Hour after hour,
With thread so very clear and fine,
   The web is like a flower.

Sometimes the lace she weaveth
   Sparkles with diamonds bright;
Sometimes 'tis covered over
   With tiny pearls so white.

---

[1] *enchased*, adorned with engraved work.

And though she weaves so tastefully,
   She is a murderess too,
Who is the lady weaver?
   Can you tell me, children, who?

* **46** *

PRETTY IS THAT PRETTY DOES.

THE spider wears a plain brown dress,
   And she is a steady spinner;
     To see her, quiet as a mouse,
     Going about her silver house,
You would never, never, never guess
   The way she gets her dinner.

She looks as if no thought of ill
   In all her life had stirred her;
     But while she moves with careful tread,
     And while she spins her silken thread,
She is planning, planning, planning still
   The way to do some murder.

My child who reads this simple lay,
   With eyes down-dropt and tender,
     Remember the old proverb says
     That pretty is that pretty does,
And that worth does not go or stay
   For poverty or splendor.

* 49 *

DUTY.

WHENE'ER you know a thing is right,
Go and do it with main [1] and might,
　　Nor let one murmur fall;
For duty makes as strong a claim
As if an angel called your name,
　　And all men heard the call.

Keep all the day, and every day,
Within the strait and narrow way,
　　And all your life, in fine; [2]
Be temperate in your moods and meats,
And in your sours and in your sweets,
　　And, lastly, don't drink wine!

* 50 *

BY-AND-BY.

THERE is a little mischief-making
　　Elfin [3] who is ever nigh,
Thwarting [4] every undertaking;
　　And his name is By-and-By.

What we ought to do this minute
　　"Will be better done," he'll cry,
"If to-morrow we begin it:"
　　"Put it off," says By-and-By.

---

[1] *main,* strength. 'Main and might' are twin synonyms.
[2] *in fine,* to sum up all. [3] *elfin,* a fairy. [4] *thwarting,* frustrating.

Those who heed the treacherous wooing [1]
    Will his faithless guidance rue; [2]
What we always put off doing
    Clearly we shall *never* do.

We shall reach what we endeavor,
    If on Now we more rely;
But unto the realms [3] of Never
    Leads the pilot By-and-By.

* 51 *

THE HONEST BIRD.

ONCE on a time a little bird
Within a wicker cage was heard,
In mournful tones, these words to sing:
" In vain I stretch my useless wing;
Still round and round I vainly fly,
And strive in vain for liberty.
Dear Liberty, how sweet thou art!"
The prisoner sings with breaking heart:
"All other things I'd give for thee,
Nor ask one joy but liberty."

He sang so sweet, a little mouse,
That often ran about the house,
Came to his cage.   Her cunning ear
She turns, the mournful bird to hear.
Soon as he ceased, "Suppose," said she,
"I could contrive to set you free,
Would you those pretty wings give me?"

---

[1] *wooing*, soliciting.   [2] *rue*, be sorry for.   [3] *realm*, kingdom.

The cage was in the window seat;
The sky was blue, the air was sweet.
The bird in eagerness replied,
"Oh, yes! my wings, and see, beside,
These seeds and apples, and sugar too! —
All, pretty mouse, I'll give to you,
If you will only set me free;
For, oh! I pant for liberty."

The mouse soon gnawed a hole. The bird,
In ecstasy, forgot his word;
Swift as an arrow, see, he flies,
Far up, far up, towards the skies;
But see! he stops, now he descends,
Towards the cage his course he bends.

"Kind mouse," said he, "behold me now
Returned to keep my foolish vow.
I only longed for freedom then,
Nor thought to want my wings again.
Better with life itself to part
Than living have a faithless heart:
Do with me, therefore, as you will,
An honest bird I will be still."

His heart seemed full, no more he said;
He drooped his wing, and hung his head.
The mouse, though very pert and smart,
Had yet a very tender heart.
She minced a little, turned about,
Then thus her sentiments spoke out: —

" I don't care much about your wings:
Apples and cakes are better things.
You love the clouds, I choose the house;
Wings would look queer upon a mouse;
My nice long tail is better far:
So keep your wings just where they are.'

She minced[1] some apples, gave a smack,
Then ran into a little crack.
The bird spread out his wings, and flew,
And vanished in the sky's deep blue;
Far up his joyful song he poured,
And sang of freedom as he soared.

* 52 *

DAYBREAK.

SEE the day begins to break,
And the light shoots like a streak
Of subtle[2] fire; the wind blows cold
While the morning doth unfold;
Now the birds begin to rouse,
And the squirrel from the boughs
Leaps, to get him nuts and fruit;
The early lark, that erst[3] was mute,
Carols in the rising day
Many a note and many a lay.

J. FLETCHER.

---

[1] *minced*, nibbled.   [2] *subtle*, rare, delicate.
[3] *erst*, before, till now.

* 53 *

CHOICE STANZAS.

**

HE prayeth best who loveth best
   All things both great and small;
For the dear God who loveth us,
   He made and loveth all.
S. T. Coleridge.

**

IF Wisdom's ways you'd wisely seek,
   Five things observe with care, —
Of whom you speak, *to* whom you speak,
   And *how*, and *when*, and *where*.

**

THE bird that soars on highest wing
   Builds on the ground her lowly nest;
And she that doth most sweetly sing
   Sings in the shade when all things rest.
     In lark and nightingale we see
     What honor hath humility.
J. Montgomery.

**

TINY threads make up the web,
   Little acts make up life's span:
Would you ever happy be,
   Spin them rightly while you can.
When the thread is broken quite,
Too late then to spin aright.

⁎

Be not false, unkind, or cruel;
Banish evil words and strife;
Keep thy heart a temple holy;
Love the lovely, aid the lowly:
Thus shall each day be a jewel
Strung upon thy thread of life.

⁎

Howe'er it be, it seems to me
　'Tis only noble to be good;
Kind hearts are more than coronets,
　And simple faith than Norman blood.

Alfred Tennyson.

⁎

The best revenge is love : — disarm
Anger with smiles; heal wounds with balm;
　Give water to thy thirsting foe :
The sandal-tree, as if to prove
How sweet to conquer hate by love,
　Perfumes the axe that lays it low.

S. C. Wilkes.

⁎

If e'er in doing aught, you dread
　Disgrace, if others know it,
Then, dearest child, the only way
　Is for you not to do it.

⁎

There's a tone in the deep
Like the murmuring breath of a lion asleep.

Eliza Cook.

* 54 *

AN HONEST NAME.

THOUGH many be more rich than we
    In all this great world's wealth by far,
We may possess a name no less
    In worth than gold or rubies are.

However hard our lot, we'll guard
    This treasure; for how great the loss,
To lose our name and honest fame,
    And only gain a little dross![1]

Though on this earth all pomp of birth
    And worldly riches may decay,
Yet every man, if honest, can
    Have wealth that none may take away.

* 55 *

SPRING–TIME.

THE Spring is come; the Spring is come!
    The brooks are merrily pouring;
And the lambs are here, and the swallows appear,
    And the lark aloft is soaring.

Old Winter is gone; old Winter is gone!
    And, pray, what prevented his stay?
Why, March was his bane;[2] and the April rain
    Has driven him quite away.

---

[1] *dross*, worthless matter, *here* gold.   [2] *bane*, harm.

Look at the birds, the dear little birds!
  They're singing on every bough,
And strain their throats with the blithest notes
  To rejoice in the sweet Spring now.

Come to the fields, away to the fields!
  We've lingered at home too long:
The sheep-bells ring as the bright birds sing,
  And the streamlet murmurs a song.

Never forget, child, never forget,
  Who it was made the world so fair,
Who with flowers and trees, and mountains and
    seas,
  Made it beautiful everywhere.

FROM THE GERMAN.

* 56 *

LAPLAND.

"WITH blue, cold nose, and wrinkled brow,
Traveller, whence comest thou?"
"From Lapland's woods and hills of frost
By the rapid reindeer crossed;
Where tapering grows the gloomy fir
And the stunted juniper;
Where the wild hare and the crow
Whiten in surrounding snow;
Where the shivering huntsmen tear
His fur coat from the grim, white bear;

Where the wolf and arctic fox
Prowl along the lonely rocks,
And tardy suns to deserts drear,
Give days and nights of half a year;[1]
From icy oceans, where the whale
Tosses in foam his lashing tail;
Where the snorting sea-horse[2] shows
His ivory teeth in grinning rows;
Where, tumbling in their seal-skin boat,
Fearless the hungry fishers float,
And from teeming[3] seas supply
The food their niggard[4] plains deny."

MISS AIKEN.

* 57 *

PUSSY'S CLASS.

"Now, children," said Puss, as she shook her head,
" It is time your morning lesson was said."
So her kittens drew near, with footsteps slow,
And sat-down before her, all in a row.

" Attention, class ! " said the cat-mamma,
" And tell me quick where your noses are."
At this all the kittens sniffed the air,
As if it were filled with a perfume[5] rare.

---

[1] Far up in the arctic region the sun does not set for six months, and then comes a night of six months.
[2] *sea-horse*, the walrus.
[3] *teeming*, full of fish.
[4] *niggard*, barren.
[5] *perfume*, a sweet odor.

"Now, what do you say when you want some
    drink?"
The kittens waited a moment to think,
And then the answer came, clear and loud —
You ought to have heard how those kittens meow'd!

"Very well! 'Tis the same, with a sharper tone,
When you want some fish, or a bit of bone.
Now what do you say when children are good?"
And the kittens purred as soft as they could.

"And what do you do when children are bad?—
When they tease and pull?" Each kitty looked
    sad.
"Pooh!" said their mother, "that isn't enough;
You must use your claws when children are rough.

"And where are your claws? No, no, my dear!"
(As she took up a paw), "see, they're hidden here."
Then all the kittens crowded about
To see their sharp little claws brought out.

"Now, 'Sptss,' as hard as you can," she said;
But every kitten hung down its head.
"'*Sptss!*' I say," cried the mother-cat,
But they said, "O mamma, we can't do that!"

"Then go and play," said the fond mamma:
"What sweet little idiots kittens are!
Ah well! I was once the same, I suppose,"
And she looked very wise, and rubbed her nose.
MARY MAPES DODGE.

* 58 *

RANGER.

A LITTLE boat in a cave,
  And a child there, fast asleep,
Floating out on a wave,
  Out to the perilous deep;
Out to the living waters
  That brightly dance and gleam,
And dash their foam about him,
  To wake him from his dream.

He rubs his pretty eyes,
  He shakes his curly head,
And says, with great surprise,
  " Why, I'm not asleep in bed!"
— The boat is rising and sinking
  Over the sailors' graves;
And he laughs out, " Isn't it nice
  Playing see-saw with the waves?"

Alas! he little thinks
  Of the grief on the far-off sands,
Where his mother trembles and shrinks,
  And his sister wrings her hands,
Watching in speechless terror
  The boat and the flaxen head.
Is there no hope of succor?
  Must they see him drowned and dead?

They see him living now, —
  Living, and jumping about;

He stands on the giddy prow,
　With a merry laugh and shout.
Oh, spare him! spare him! spare him!
　Spare him, thou cruel deep!
— The child is swept from the prow,
　And the wild waves dance and leap.

They run to the edge of the shore,
　They stretch their arms to him;
Knee-deep they wade, and more;
　But alas! they cannot swim.
Their pretty, pretty darling!
　His little hat floats by;
They see his frightened face,
　They hear his drowning cry.

Something warm and strong
　Dashes before them then,
Hairy and curly and long,
　And brave as a dozen men;
Bounding, panting, gasping,
　Rushing straight as a dart;
Ready to die in the cause, —
　A dog with a loyal heart!

He fights with the fighting sea,
　He grandly wins his prize;
Mother! he brings it thee
　With triumph in his eyes.
He brings it thee, O mother!
　His burden, pretty and pale;

He lays it down at thy feet,
And wags his honest old tail.

O dog so faithful and bold!
O dog so tender and true!
You shall wear a collar of gold,
And a crown, if you like it, too.
O Ranger! in love and honor,
Your name shall be handed down,
And children's hearts shall beat
At the story of your renown!

POEMS FOR A CHILD.

* 59 *

GRANDPAPA.

GRANDPAPA'S hair is very white,
And grandpapa walks but slow;
He likes to sit still in his easy-chair
While the children come and go.
"Hush! play quietly," says mamma;
"Let nobody trouble dear grandpapa."

Grandpapa's hand is thin and weak,
It has worked hard all his days,—
A strong right hand, and an honest hand, .
That has won all good men's praise.
"Kiss it tenderly," says mamma;
"Let every one honor grandpapa."

Grandpapa's eyes are growing dim,
They have looked on sorrow and death;

But the love-light never went out of them,
　　Nor the courage and the faith.
" You, children, all of you," says mamma,
" Have need to look up to dear grandpapa."

Grandpapa's years are wearing few,
　　But he leaves a blessing behind, —
A good life lived and a good fight fought,
　　True heart and equal [1] mind.
" Remember, my children," says mamma,
" You bear the name of your grandpapa."

Dinah Muloch Craik.

· * 60 *

A CHILD'S EVENING HYMN.

How beautiful the setting sun !
　　The clouds, how bright and gay !
The stars, appearing one by one,
　　How beautiful are they !

And when the moon climbs up the sky,
　　And sheds her gentle light,
And hangs her crystal [2] lamp on high,
　　How beautiful is night !

And can it be I am possessed
　　Of something brighter far ?
Glows there a light within this breast
　　Outshining every star ?

---

[1] *equal*, not variable, even.　　[2] *crystal*, bright like a clear kind of glass.

Yes; should the sun and stars turn pale,
    The mountains melt away,
This flame within shall never fail,
    But live in endless day.

This is the soul that God has given;
    Sin may its lustre [1] dim,
While goodness bears it up to heaven,
    And leads it back to Him.

Mrs. Follen.

* 61 *

CHILD-FAITH.

By Alpine lake, 'neath shady rock,
The herd-boy knelt beside his flock,
And softly told, with pious air,
His A, B, C, as evening prayer.

Unseen, the pastor lingered near;
"My child, what means the sound I hear?"

"Where'er the hills and valleys blend,
The sound of prayer and praise ascend;
Must I not in the worship share,
And raise to Heaven my evening prayer?"

"My child, a prayer that ne'er can be: -
You have but [2] said your A, B, C."

---

[1] *lustre*, brightness.   [2] *but*, only.

"I have no better way to pray,
But all I know to God I say;
I tell the letters on my knees,
And He'll make words Himself to please."

S. W. LANDER. — *From the German.*

* 62 *

THE OLD PROVERB.

" THE boy is father to the man : "
  Such talk sounds very queer to me ;
But I suppose they mean to say,
  If I a true, brave man would be,
I must not be a sneaking boy,
  But in my work, or in my play,
Whatever I may say or do,
  Be true and honest as the day.

" The boy is father to the man : "
  I wonder how it is with girls !
If all they care for is to be
  Pretty and fair, with glossy curls,
And handsome dresses, will they grow
  To noble women, good and true ?
Or will they be like pretty dolls,
  Which please us for an hour or two ?

" The boy is father to the man : "
  Then, boys and girls, suppose we look
For the best pattern we can find,
  And take him for our copy-book.

Then, looking backward, we may see
A pleasant pathway clear and bright,
And, looking forward, we may hope
To reach the World of Light.

EFFIE JOHNSON.

* 63 *

DAFFY–DOWN–DILLY.

I.

DAFFY-DOWN-DILLY
Came up in the cold,
Through the brown mould,
Although the March breezes
Blew keen on her face,
Although the white snow
Lay on many a place.

Daffy-down-dilly
Had heard under ground
The sweet rushing sound
Of the streams, as they broke
From their white winter chains,
Of the whistling spring winds,
And the pattering rains.

"Now, then," thought Daffy,
Deep down in her heart,
"It's time I should start."

So she pushed her soft leaves
 Through the hard frozen ground,
Quite up to the surface,
 And then she looked round.

There was snow all about her,
 Gray clouds overhead;
The trees all looked dead:
Then how do you think
 Poor Daffy-down felt,
When the sun would not shine,
 And the ice would not melt?

II.

" Cold weather!" thought Daffy,
 Still working away;
" The earth's hard to-day!
There's but a half inch
 Of my leaves to be seen,
And two thirds of that
 Is more yellow than green.

"I can't do much yet;
 But I'll do what I can:
 It's well I began!
For, unless I can manage
 To lift up my head,
The people will think
 That the Spring herself's dead."

So, little by little,
  She brought her leaves out,
  All clustered about ;
And then her bright flowers
  Began to unfold,
Till Daffy stood robed
  In her spring green and gold.

O Daffy-down-dilly,
  So brave and so true !
  I wish all were like you ! —
So ready for duty
  In all sorts of weather,
And loyal to courage
  And duty together.

Miss Warner.

* 64 *

DOING GOOD.

WHAT if a drop of rain should plead,
  "So small a drop as I
Can ne'er refresh the thirsty mead,[1]
  I'll tarry in the sky " ?

What if a single beam of noon
  Should in its fountain stay,
Because its feeble light alone
  Cannot create a day?

[1] *mead*, meadow.

Does not each rain-drop help to form
  The cool refreshing shower?
And every ray of light to warm
  And beautify [1] the flower?

Go, thou, and strive to do thy share;
  One talent, — less than thine, —
Improved with steady zeal and care,
  Would gain rewards divine.

* 65 *

THE RIVER.

RIVER, River, little River!
Bright you sparkle on your way,
O'er the yellow pebbles dancing,
Through the flowers and foliage [2] glancing,
  Like a child at play.

River, River, swelling River!
On you rush o'er rough and smooth, —
Louder, faster, brawling, leaping
Over rocks, by meadows sweeping, —
  Like impetuous [3] youth.

River, River, brimming River!
Broad and deep, and still as time,

---

[1] *beautify*, make beautiful.   [2] *foliage*, green leaves.
[3] *impetuous*, hasty, violent.

Seeming *still*, yet still in motion,
Tending onward to the ocean,
    Just like mortal prime.[1]

River, River, rapid River!
Swifter now you slip away, —
Swift and silent as an arrow,
Through a channel dark and narrow,
    Like life's closing day.

River, River, headlong River!
Down you dash into the sea, —
Sea, that line hath never sounded,
Sea, that voyage hath never rounded,[2]
    Like Eternity.

* 66 *

THE WORLD.

GREAT, wide, beautiful, wonderful World,
With the wonderful water around you curled,
And the wonderful grass on your breast —
World, you are beautifully dressed.

The wonderful air is over me,
And the wonderful wind is shaking the tree;
It walks on the water, and whirls the mills,
And talks to itself on the tops of the hills.

---

[1] *mortal prime*, man in his prime.
[2] *rounded*, crossed and returned.

You friendly Earth, how far do you go,
With the wheat-fields that nod, and the rivers
    that flow,
With cities, and gardens, and cliffs, and isles,
And people upon you for thousands of miles?

Ah! you are so great, and I am so small,
I tremble to think of you, World, at all;
And yet, when I said my prayers to-day,
A whisper inside me seemed to say,
"You are more than the Earth, though you are
    such a dot:
You can love and think, and the Earth cannot!"

MATTHEW BROWNE.

* 67 *

A LITTLE GIRL'S FANCIES.

O LITTLE flowers, you love me so,
    You could not do without me;
O little birds that come and go,
    You sing sweet songs about me;
O little moss, observed[1] by few,
    That round the tree is creeping,
You like my head to rest on you
    When I am idly sleeping.

O rushes by the river side,
    You bow when I come near you;

---

[1] *observed*, noticed.

* 70 *

RAIN IN SUMMER.

O GENTLE, gentle summer rain,
   Let not the silver lily pine,
The drooping lily pine in vain,
   To feel that dewy touch of thine,
To drink thy freshness once again,
O gentle, gentle summer rain!

In heat the landscape quivering lies;
   The cattle pant beneath the tree;
Through parching air and purple skies
   The Earth looks up in vain for thee;
For thee, for thee, it looks in vain,
O gentle, gentle summer rain!

Come, thou, and brim the meadow streams,
   And soften all the hills with mist,
O falling dew! from burning dreams
   By thee shall herb and flower be kissed;
And Earth shall bless thee yet again,
O gentle, gentle summer rain!
                                   W. C. BENNETT.

* 71 *

AFTER A STORM.

WITH a freshness and sweetness
   The air is made new;
The birds are all singing;
   The skies are all blue;

The flowers have uplifted
Their petals[1] again ;
And the meadows grow green
At the touch of the rain.

DORA READ GOODALE.
(In "Apple Blossoms.")

* 72 *

SEVEN TIMES ONE. — EXULTATION.

THERE'S no dew left on the daisies and clover,
　There's no rain left in heaven ;
I've said my " seven times " over and over —
　Seven times one are seven.

I am old ! so old I can write a letter ;
　My birthday lessons are done :
The lambs play always, they know no better ;
　They are only one times one.

O Moon ! in the night I have seen you sailing,
　And shining so round and low ;
You were bright ! ah, bright ! but your light is
　　　failing ;
　You are nothing now but a bow.

You Moon ! have you done something wrong in
　　　heaven,
　That God has hidden your face ?
I hope, if you have, you will soon be forgiven,
　And shine again in your place.

---

[1] *petals*, leaves.

O velvet Bee ! you're a dusty fellow,
   You've powdered your legs with gold;
O brave marsh Mary-buds, rich and yellow!
   Give me your money to hold.

O Columbine ! open your folded wrapper
   Where two twin turtle-doves dwell;
O Cuckoo-pint ! toll me the purple clapper,
   That hangs in your clear, green bell.

And show me your nest with the young ones in it—
   I will not steal them away,
I am old ! you may trust me, Linnet, Linnet, —
   I am seven times one to-day.

JEAN INGELOW.

* 73 *

HIAWATHA'S HUNTING.

THEN the little Hiawatha
Learned of every bird its language,
Learned their names and all their secrets, —
How they built their nests in summer,
Where they hid themselves in winter;
Talked with them where'er he met them,
Called them " Hiawatha's Chickens."

Of all beasts he learned the language,
Learned their names and all their secrets, —
How the beavers built their lodges,

Where the squirrels hid their acorns,
How the reindeer ran so swiftly,
Why the rabbit was so timid;
Talked with them where'er he met them,
Called them " Hiawatha's Brothers."

Then Iagoo, the great boaster,
He, the marvellous story-teller,
He, the traveller and the talker,
Made a bow for Hiawatha;
From a branch of ash he made it;
From an oak bough made the arrows,
Tipped with flint, and winged with feathers;
And the cord he made of deer-skin.

Then he said to Hiawatha:
" Go, my son, into the forest,
Where the red deer herd together;
Kill for us a famous roebuck,
Kill for us a deer with antlers." [1]

Forth into the forest straightway
All alone walked Hiawatha
Proudly, with his bow and arrows;
And the birds sang round him, o'er him,
" Do not shoot us, Hiawatha!"
Sang the robin, sang the bluebird,
" Do not shoot us, Hiawatha!"

Up the oak-tree, close beside him,
Sprang the squirrel, lightly leaping

antlers, branches of a stag's horn.

In and out among-the branches;
Coughed and chattered from the oak-tree,
Laughed, and said between his laughing,
" Do not shoot me, Hiawatha!"

And the rabbit from his pathway
Leaped aside, and at a distance
Sat erect upon his haunches,
Half in fear, and half in frolic,
Saying to the little hunter,
" Do not shoot me, Hiawatha!"

But he heeded not, nor heard them,
For his thoughts were with the red deer;
On their tracks his eyes were fastened,
Leading downward to the river,
To the ford across the river,
And as one in slumber walked he.

Hidden in the alder bushes,
There he waited till the deer came,
Till he saw two antlers lifted,
Saw two eyes look from the thicket,
Saw two nostrils point to windward,
And a deer came down the pathway,
Flecked with leafy light and shadow.
And his heart within him fluttered,
Trembled like the leaves above him,
Like the birch leaf palpitated,[1]
As the deer came down the pathway.

---

[1] *palpitated*, throbbed, fluttered.

Then, upon one knee·uprising,
Hiawatha aimed an arrow;
Scarce a twig moved with his motion,
Scarce a leaf was stirred or rustled;
But the wary roebuck started,
Stamped with all his hoofs together,
Listened with one foot uplifted,
Leaped as if to meet the arrow;
Ah, the singing, fatal arrow!
Like a wasp, it buzzed, and stung him.

Dead he lay there in the forest,
By the ford across the river;
Beat his timid heart no longer:
But the heart of Hiawatha
Throbbed and shouted and exulted
As he bore the red deer homeward.

H. W. LONGFELLOW.

* 74 *

GOD'S LOVE FOR ALL.

GOD made the pleasant summer,
    The fruits that round us fall,
The sunny skies, the streams, the birds, —
    God made them for us all.

He did not make the sunbeams gild
    Alone the rich man's door;
Oh, no!   He blessed with light alike
    The wealthy and the poor.

He made the pretty flowers
. To blossom wild and free;
He did not make them that the great
Alone their smiles should see.

Oh, no! He made them for us all,
To bless this land of ours;
And, more than that, He gave us love
Wherewith to love the flowers.

Yes, God upon his children smiles,
No matter when or where;
He sees them in the pleasant fields,
And smiles upon them there.

Alike for all His love descends,
No matter what their lot, —
The wealthy in their stately halls,
The peasant [1] in his cot.

* 75 *

SUNSHINE AND SHOWER.

I.

Two children stood at their father's gate, —
Two girls with golden hair;
And their eyes were bright, and their voices glad,
Because the morn was fair.
For they said, " We will take that long, long walk
To the hawthorn copse [2] to-day,

---

[1] *peasant*, poor man.　　[2] *copse*, a wood of small growth.

And gather great bunches of lovely flowers
   From off the scented may; [1]
And oh! we shall be so happy there,
   'Twill be sorrow to come away."

As the children spoke, a little cloud
   Passed slowly across the sky;
And one looked up in her sister's face
   With a tear-drop in her eye.
But the other said, " Oh! heed it not;
   'Tis far too fair to rain;
That little cloud may search the sky
   For other clouds in vain."
And soon the children's voices rose
   In merriment again.

But, ere the morning hours had waned,
   The sky had changed its hue,
And that one cloud had chased away
   The whole great heaven of blue.
The rain fell down in heavy drops;
   The wind began to blow;
And the children, in their nice warm room,
   Went fretting to and fro;
For they said, " When we have aught in store, [2]
   It always happens so."

II.

Now these two fair-haired sisters
   Had a brother out at sea, —

---

[1] *may*, hawthorn blossom (of May).
[2] *aught in store*, any thing pleasant to do.

A little midshipman [1] aboard
  The gallant "/Victory;"
And on that self-same morning
  When they stood beside the gate,
His ship was wrecked, and on a raft
  He stood all desolate,
With the other sailors round him,
  Prepared to meet their fate.

Beyond, they saw the cool green land, —
  The land with its waving trees,
And the little brooks that rise and fall
  Like butterflies to the breeze;
And above them the burning noontide sun
  With scorching stillness shone;
Their throats were parched with bitter thirst,
  And they knelt down one by one,
Praying to God for a drop of rain,
  And a gale to waft them on.

Just then that little cloud was sent, —
  That shower in mercy given;
And, as a bird before the breeze,
  Their bark was landward driven.
Now, some few mornings after,
  When the children met once more,
And their brother told the story,
  They knew it was the hour
When they had wished for sunshine,
  And God had sent the shower.

---

[1] *midshipman*, a naval officer lower in rank than a lieutenant.

* 76 *

MOTES IN THE SUNBEAMS.

THE motes up and down in the sun
  Ever restlessly moving we see;
Whereas the great mountains stand still,
  Unless terrible earthquakes there be.

If these atoms that move up and down
  Were useful as restless they are,
Than a mountain I rather would be
  A mote in the sunbeam so fair.

CHARLES AND MARY LAMB.
(In " Poetry for Children.")

* 77 *

BOYS' PLAY AND GIRLS' PLAY.

"Now, let's have a game of play, —
Lucy, Jane, and little May, —
I will be a grizzly bear,
Prowling here and prowling there,
Sniffing round and round about,
Till I find you children out;
And my dreadful den shall be
Deep within the hollow tree."

"Oh, no! please not, Robert dear;
Do not be a grizzly bear!
Little May was half afraid
When she heard the noise you made,

Roaring like a lion strong,
Just now, as you came along;
And she'll scream and start to-night,
If you give her any fright."

" Well, then I'll be a fox :
You shall be the hens and cocks
In the farmer's apple-tree
Crowing out so lustily.
I will softly creep this way, —
Peep, and pounce upon my prey;
And I'll bear you to my den,
Where the fern grows in the glen."

" Oh, no, Robert! you're so strong,
While you're dragging us along
I'm afraid you'll tear our frocks:
We won't play at hens and cocks."
" If you won't play fox or bears,
I'm a dog, and you be hares;
Then you'll only have to run —
Girls are never up to fun."

" You've your play, and we have ours;
Go, and climb the trees again!
I and little May and Jane
Are so happy with our flowers!
Jane is culling foxglove bells;
May and I are making posies,
And we want to search the dells
For the latest summer roses."

MRS. HAWTREY.

* 78 *

MR. NOBODY.

I KNOW a funny little man,
  As quiet as a mouse,
Who does the mischief that is done
  In everybody's house.
There's no one ever sees his face;
  And yet we all agree
That every plate we break was cracked
  By Mr. Nobody.

'Tis he who always tears our books,
  Who leaves the door ajar;
He pulls the buttons from our skirts,
  And scatters pins afar.
That squeaking door will always squeak;
  For, prithee, don't you see,
We leave the oiling to be done
  By Mr. Nobody?

He puts damp wood upon the fire,
  That kettles cannot boil;
His are the feet that bring in mud,
  And all the carpets soil.
The papers always are mislaid:
  Who had them last but he?
There's no one tosses them about
  But Mr. Nobody.

* 83 *

THE NOBLE MAN.

I LOVE the man who freely gives
  As Heaven has blest his store;
Who shares the gifts that he receives
  With those who need them more;
Whose melting heart of pity moves
  For sorrow and distress;
Of all his friends, who mostly loves
  The poor, the fatherless.

I love the man who scorns to be
  To name or sect a slave;
Whose soul is like the sunshine, free,
  Free as the ocean wave;
Who, when he sees oppression, wrong,
  Speaks out in thunder tones;
Who feels, with Truth, that he is strong
  To grapple e'en with thrones.

I love the man who shuns to do
  An action mean or low;
Who will a noble course pursue
  To stranger, friend, and foe;
Who seeks for justice, not for gain;
  Is merciful and kind;
Who will not give a needless pain
  In body or in mind.

I love the man whose only pride
  Is wisdom, virtue, right;
Who feels, if truth is e'er denied,
  His honor has a blight;
Who ne'er evades by look or sign —
  In weal or woe the same:
Methinks the glories are divine
  Which cluster round his name.

D. C. COLESWORTHY.

* 84 *

WISHES AND REALITIES.

A CHILD'S WISHES.

I WISH I were a little bird,
  To fly so far and high,
And sail along the golden clouds,
  And through the azure [1] sky!
I'd be the first to see the sun
  Up from the ocean spring;
And, ere it [2] touched the glittering spire, [3]
  His ray should gild my wing.

Above the hills I'd watch him still,
  Far down the crimson west,
And sing to him my evening song
  Ere yet I sought my rest;

---

[1] *azure* (ā'zhur), of a delicate blue color.
[2] *ere it*, before it, that is, the sun's ray mentioned in the next line.
[3] *spire*, the upper, tapering part of a church steeple.

And many a land I then should see,
  As hill and plain I crossed ;
Nor fear, through all the pathless sky,
  That I should e'er be lost.

I'd fly where, round the olive bough,
  The vine its tendrils weaves,
And shelter from the noonbeams seek
  Among the myrtle leaves.
Now if I climb our highest hill,
  How little can I see !
Oh had I but a pair of wings,
· How happy should I be !

REPLY.

Wings cannot soar above the sky,
  As thou *in thought* canst do ;
Nor can the veiling clouds confine
  Thy mental eye's [1] keen view ;
Not to the sun dost thou chant forth
  Thy simple evening hymn : ·
Thou praisest Him before whose smile
  The noonday sun grows dim.

But thou mayst learn to trace the sun
  Around the earth and sky,
And see him rising, setting still
  Where distant oceans lie ;

---

[1] *mental eye*, that is, the mind, which may figuratively be said to *see* what it thinks about.

To other lands the bird may guide
 His pinions through the air:
Ere yet he rest his wings, thou art,
 In *thought*, before him there.

Though strong and free, his wing may droop,
 Or bands restrain his flight;
THOUGHT none may stay — more fleet its course
 Than swiftest beams of light.
A lovelier clime than birds can find,
 While summers go and come,
Beyond this earth remains for those
 Whom God doth summon home.

* 85 *

GENTLE DEEDS.

'Tis better far one breast to cheer
 Than bear a hero's name;
To heal one heart, or dry a tear,
 Is sweeter far than fame.

To shield the right, the wrong prevent,
 To take away a pain,
To love the pure and innocent,
 Are noblest traits of men.

With all the fame of battle-fields
 That smoke with human blood,
A gentle deed an incense yields
 That rises nearer God.

When but a little piece of bread
　　To one who needs is given,
Though history may not mark the deed,
　　'Tis chronicled[1] in heaven.

H. P. BIDDLE.

* 86 *

THE LAW OF CHARITY.

OH! never let us lightly fling
　　A barb[2] of woe to wound another;
Oh! never let us haste to bring
　　The cup of sorrow to a brother.

Each has the power to wound; but he
　　Who wounds that he may witness pain
Has spurned the law of charity,
　　Which ne'er inflicts a pang in vain.

'Tis godlike to awaken joy,
　　Or sorrow's influence to subdue;
But not to wound or to annoy
　　Is part of virtue's lesson too.

Peace, winged in fairer worlds above,
　　Shall lend her dawn to brighten this;
Then all man's labor shall be love,
　　And all his aim his brother's bliss.

T. GISBORNE.

[1] *chronicled*, recorded, known.
[2] *barb*, the sharp shoulders of an arrow-head.

When a band of exiles moored their bark
On the wild New England shore.

p. 3-

Select Poetry for Young Folks.

* 1 *

THE TREE.

THE Tree's early leaf-buds were bursting their
  brown:
"Shall I take them away?" said the Frost, sweep-
  ing down.
"No, leave them alone
Till the blossoms have grown,"
Prayed the Tree, while he trembled from rootlet[1]
  to crown.

The Tree bore his blossoms, and all the birds
  sung:
"Shall I take them away?" said the Wind as he
  swung.
"No, leave them alone
Till the berries have grown,"
Said the Tree, while his leaflets[2] quivering hung.

---

[1] *rootlet*, little root.   [2] *leaflet*, little leaf.

3

The Tree bore his fruit in the midsummer glow:
Said the girl, " May I gather thy berries now ? "
    " Yes, all thou canst see ;
    Take them : all are for thee,"
Said the Tree, while he bent down his laden boughs
    low.
               BJÖRNSTJERNE BJÖRNSON.

∗ 2 ∗

UNDER THE GREENWOOD TREE.

UNDER the greenwood tree [1]
Who [2] loves to lie with me,
And tune his merry note
Unto the sweet bird's throat,
Come hither, come hither, come hither !
    Here shall we see
    No enemy
But winter and rough weather.

Who [2] doth ambition shun,
And loves to live i' the sun [3]
Seeking the food he eats,
And pleased with what he gets,
Come hither, come hither, come hither !
    Here shall he see
    No enemy
But winter and rough weather.
               W. SHAKESPEARE.

[1] *greenwood tree*, a tree with the green leaves out.   [2] he who.
[3] *i' the sun*, in the sunshine.

But not alone to plant and bird
  That little stream was known ;
Its gentle murmur far was heard,
  A friend's familiar tone ;
It glided by the cotter's [1] door,
It blessed the labors of the poor.

And would that I could thus be found,
  While travelling life's brief way,
A humble friend to all around,
  Where'er my footsteps stray, —
Like that pure stream, with tranquil breast,
Like it still blessing and still blest.

M. A. STODART.

* 5 *

A LILY'S WORD.

MY delicate Lily,
  Blossom of fragrant snow,
Breathing on me from the garden,
  How does your beauty grow ?
Tell me what blessing the kind heavens give !
How do you find it so sweet to live ?

One loving smile of the sun
  Charms me out of the mould ;
One tender tear of the rain
  Makes my full heart unfold.

[1] *cotter*, one who lives in a cot, or small house.

Welcome whatever the kind heavens give,
And you shall find it as sweet to live.

* 6 *

THE TIGER.

TIGER, tiger, burning bright
In the forest of the night,
What immortal hand or eye
Could frame thy fearful symmetry?[1]

In what distant deeps or skies
Burned the ardor of thine eyes?
On what wings dare he aspire, —
What the hand dare seize the fire?

And what shoulder, and what art
Could twist the sinews of thy heart?
And, when thy heart began to beat,
What dread hand formed thy dread feet?

What the hammer, what the chain,
In what furnace was thy brain? —
Did God smile his work to see?
Did He who made the lamb make thee?

W. BLAKE.

[1] *symmetry*, beauty of form.

* 7 *

THE EAGLE.

HE clasps the crag with hookéd hands;
Close to the sun in lonely lands,
Ringed with the azure world, he stands.

The wrinkled sea beneath him crawls;
He watches from his mountain walls,
And like a thunderbolt he falls.

ALFRED TENNYSON.

* 8 *

THE LION.

LION, thou art girt with might,
King by uncontested right;
Strength and majesty and pride
Are in thee personified.
Slavish doubt, or timid fear,
Never came thy spirit near:
What it is to fly, or bow
To a mightier than thou
Never has been known to thee,
Creature, terrible and free!

Power the mightiest gave the lion
Sinews like to bands of iron,
Gave him force which never failed,
Gave a heart that never quailed.

Triple-mailéd [1] coat of steel,
Plates of brass from head to heel,
Less defensive were [2] in wearing
Than the lion's heart of daring;
Nor could towers of strength impart
Trust like that which keeps his heart.

When he sends his roaring forth,
Silence falls upon the earth;
For the creatures great and small
Know his terror-breathing call,
And, as if by death pursued,
Leave to him a solitude.

Lion, thou art made to dwell
In hot lands, intractable,
And thyself, the sun, the sand,
Are a tyrannous triple band: [3]
Lion, King, and desert throne,
All the region is your own!

MARY HOWITT

[1] 'a coat of mail' is defensive armor for the body, formed of a network of steel rings or plates.
[2] *were*, would be.
[3] a threefold band of tyrants, — three tyrants.

* 9 *

I CAN AND I WILL.

I CAN! — he is a fiery youth,
  And WILL, a brother twin;
And, arm in arm, in love and truth,
  They'll either die or win.

Shoulder to shoulder, ever ready,
  All firm and fearless still,
The brothers labor, true and steady, —
  I CAN, and brave I WILL.

I CAN climbs to the mountain top,
  And ploughs the billowy main;[1]
He lifts the hammer in the shop,
  And drives the saw and plane.

Then say "*I can!*" Yes, let it ring;
  There is a volume[2] there:
There's meaning in the eagle's wing:
  Then soar, and *do*, and DARE.

Oh, banish from you every " *Can't*,"
  And show yourself a man;
And nothing will your purpose daunt,
  Led by the brave I CAN.

---

[1] *main*, ocean or main sea.   [2] *volume*, power.

* 10 *

CASABIANCA.[1]

A TRUE STORY.

THE boy stood on the burning deck,
　Whence all but he had fled;
The flame that lit the battle's wreck
　Shone round him o'er the dead:
Yet beautiful and bright he stood
　As born to rule the storm!
A creature of heroic blood,
　A proud, though childlike form!

The flames rolled on — he would not go
　Without his father's word:
That father, faint in death below,
　His voice no longer heard.
He called aloud: "Say, father, say
　If yet my task is done!"
He knew not that the chieftain lay
　Unconscious of his son.

"Speak, father!" once again he cried,
　"If I may yet be gone!"
And but[2] the booming[3] shots replied,
　And fast the flames rolled on.

---

[1] Casablanca was son to a French Admiral commanding the flag-ship *L'Orient* at the battle of the Nile, 1798.
　[2] *but*, only.　　　　[3] *booming*, deep sounding.

Upon his brow he felt their breath,
  And in his waving hair,
And looked from that lone post of death
  In still yet brave despair;

And shouted but once more aloud,
  "My father! must I stay?"
While o'er him fast, through sail and shroud,
  The wreathing fires made way.
They wrapt the ship in splendor wild,
  They caught the flag on high,
And streamed above the gallant child,
  Like banners in the sky.

There came a burst of thunder-sound —
  The boy — oh! where was he?
Ask of the winds that far around
  With fragments strewed the sea, —
With mast, and helm, and pennon [1] fair,
  That well had borne their part;
But the noblest thing which perished there
  Was that young faithful heart!

                              MRS. FELICIA HEMANS.

* 11 *

ROME WASN'T BUILT IN A DAY.

THE boy who does a stroke, and stops,
  Will ne'er a great man be:
'Tis the aggregate [2] of single drops
  That makes the sea the sea.

---

[1] *pennon*, small flag.   [2] *aggregate*, whole amount, mass.

The mountain was not at its birth
    A mountain, so to speak:
The little atoms of sand and earth
    Have made its peak a peak.

Not all at once the morning streams,[1]
    The gold above the gray:
'Tis thousand little yellow gleams
    That makes the day the day.

Not from the snow-drift, May awakes,
    In purples, reds, and greens;
Spring's whole bright retinue[2] it takes
    To make her queen of queens.

Upon the orchard, rain must fall,
    And soak from branch to root,
And blossoms bloom and fade withal,
    Before the fruit is fruit.

The farmer needs must sow and till,
    And wait the wheaten bread;
Then cradle, thrash, and go to mill,
    Before the bread is bread.

Swift heels may get the early shout,
    But, spite of all the din,
It is the patient *holding out*
    That makes the winner win.

---

[1] *streams*, emits streams of light.   [2] *retinue*, train of followers.

Make this your motto, then, at start,
'Twill help to smooth the way,
And steady up both hand and heart, —
" Rome wasn't built in a day ! "

ALICE CARY.

* 12 *

LITTLE BY LITTLE.

ONE step, and then another,
And the longest walk is ended;
One stitch, and then another,
And the largest rent is mended;
One brick upon another,
And the highest wall is made;
One flake upon another,
And the deepest snow is laid.

So the little coral-workers,[1]
By their slow but constant motion,
Have built those pretty islands
In the distant dark-blue ocean;
And the noblest undertakings
Man's wisdom hath conceived,[2]
By oft repeated efforts
Have been patiently achieved.[3]

---

[1] *coral*, a hard limy substance of various colors. It is really the skeletons
of a kind of animal resembling plants or flowers. In some warm latitudes
of the ocean they have formed coral-reefs or coral islands.

[2] *conceived*, planned.   [3] *achieved*, done.

Then do not look disheartened
   O'er the work you have to do,
And say that such a mighty task
   You never can get through,
But just endeavor day by day
   Another point to gain,
And soon the mountain which you feared
   Will prove to be a plain.

" Rome was not builded in a day,"
   The ancient proverb teaches;
And Nature, by her trees and flowers,
   The same sweet sermon preaches.
Think not of far-off duties,
   But of duties which are near,
And, having once begun to work,
   Resolve to persevere.

* 13 *

I–HAVE AND O–HAD–I;

OR, A BIRD IN HAND IS WORTH TWO IN THE BUSH.

THERE are two little songsters well known in the
   land,
   Their names are I-Have and O-Had-I;
I-Have will come tamely and perch on your
   hand,
   But O-Had-I will mock you most sadly.

A story of a dim ravine
O'er which the towering tree-tops lean,
With one blue rift of sky between:

And there, two thousand years ago,
A little flower as white as snow
Swayed in the silence to and fro.

Day after day, with longing eye,
The floweret watched the narrow sky,
And fleecy clouds that floated by.

And through the darkness, night by night,
One gleaming star would climb the height,
And cheer the lonely floweret's sight.

Thus watching the blue heavens afar,
And the rising of its favorite star,
A slow change came, — but not to mar:

For softly o'er its petals [1] white
There crept a blueness, like the light
Of skies upon a summer night;

And in its chalice,[2] I am told,
The bonny [3] bell was formed to hold
A tiny star, that gleamed like gold.

---

[1] *pet'als*, leaves.   [2] *chalice* (chal'is), cup, flower-cup.
[3] *bonny*, beautiful.

Now, little people sweet and true,
I find a lesson here for you,
Writ in the floweret's bell of blue:

The patient child whose watchful eye
Strives after all things pure and high
Shall take their image by and by.

＊ 16 ＊

THE BARLEY–MOWERS' SONG.

BARLEY-MOWERS, here we stand,
One, two, three, a steady band,
True of heart and strong of limb,
Ready in our harvest trim ;
All a-row, with spirits blithe,
. Now we whet the bended scythe,
Rink-a-tink, rink-a-tink, rink-a-tink-a-tink !

Side by side, now bending low,
Down the swaths of barley go,
Stroke by stroke, as true's [1] the chime
Of the bells, we keep in time ;
Then we whet the ringing scythe, ·
Standing 'mong the barley lithe,[2]
Rink-a-tink, rink-a-tink, rink-a-tink-a-tink.

---

[1] *as true's*, as true as.　　　[2] *lithe*, easily bent.

* 18 *

THE BUILDING OF THE NEST.

THEY'LL come again to the apple-tree, —
Robin and all the rest, —
When the orchard branches are fair to see
In the snow of the blossoms dressed ;
And the prettiest thing in the world will be
The building of the nest.

Weaving it well, so round and trim,
Hollowing it with care ;
Nothing too far away for him,
Nothing for her too fair ;
Hanging it safe on the topmost limb, —
Their castle in the air.

Ah, mother-bird, you'll have weary days
When the eggs are under your breast,
And your mate will fear for wilful ways
When the wee ones leave the nest ;
But they'll find their wings in a glad amaze,
And God will see to the rest.

So come to the trees with all your train
When the apple blossoms blow ;
Through the April shimmer of sun and rain
Go flying to and fro ;
And sing to our hearts as we watch again
Your fairy building grow.

MRS. M. E. SANGSTER.

* 19 *

CLEANLINESS.

ALL endearing cleanliness,
Virtue next to godliness,
Easiest, cheapest, needful'st duty,
To the body health and beauty:
Who that's human would refuse it,
When a little water does it?

CHARLES AND MARY LAMB
(In " *Poetry for Children* ")

* 20 *

LADY TABBYSKIN'S BALL.

LADY Tabbyskin gave a large party last night,
　While we were asleep in our beds;
The pussy-cats danced in the clear moonlight,
　All over the tiles[1] and leads.

Sir Grimalkin[2] the Fierce, just home from the
　wars,
　And Mademoiselle[3] Minette, from France, —
You'd never suspect such a darling had claws, —
　Led off in the first country-dance.[4]

---

[1] *tile*, a piece of baked clay used for roofing.
[2] *Grimalkin* (gri măl'kin), a name given to an old cat.
[3] *Mademoiselle*, Miss.
[4] *country-dance*, a dance in which the partners are arranged in opposite lines — rightly *contra-dance*.

Sweet Blanchette was there, blue eyes and white
  hair,
The belle of the country all round ;
But so deaf, that, though all were meowing for her,
She never could hear the first sound.

Black Tom gazed and sighed, as if deeply in love ;
He looked somewhat anxious and pale ;
But, just as he hoped the fair creature to move,
Slyboots gave a tug at his tail.

Miss Tortoise-shell [1] sang a most beautiful song,
  Though I could not quite make out the words ;
But the pith of the ditty,[2] unless I heard wrong,
  Was tender young mice and sweet birds.

They all joined in chorus — oh, dear ! oh, dear !
  It woke me up out of my sleep :
Such music it never befell me to hear !
  — I ran to the window to peep ;

And there I beheld — a sweet picture to see —
  Pussy-cats big, and pussy-cats small,
As they danced and they sang on the roofs in high
  glee,
  At the great Lady Tabbyskin's ball !

MRS. CHARLES HEATON

---

[1] *Tortoise-shell* (tor'tiz), the shell of a kind of sea-turtle. The reference
here is to the color.
[2] *pith of the ditty,* meaning of the song.

* 21 *

THE SORROWFUL SEA-GULL.

The Sea-gull is *so* sorry!
   She flings herself about,
And utters little wailing cries,
   And flutters in and out.

The fishes do not sympathize —
   Fish are so very cool!
They make so many rules, you know
   And who can *feel* by rule?

They have a rule for swimming,
   A rule for taking food;
They have a rule for pleasure trips,
   A rule for doing good.

And people who make rules like that
   May dine, and work, and swim,
But never know how sweet a thing
   It is to take a whim.

I'd like to be a Sea-gull,
   With lovely beak and claws;
I would not like to be a Fish,
   Subject to fishy laws.

And, if they make more changes soon
   By acts of parliament,
I won't consent to be a fish, —
   I *never will* consent!

Why is the Sea-gull sorry?
I'm not allowed to tell.
The fish, who will not sympathize,
Know what's the matter well!

And you who'd feel with all your hearts,
And give her love and tears,
Are not allowed to hear a word —
And such is life, my dears!

CHILD-WORLD.

* 22 *

THE LITTLE GIRL'S FAWN.

WITH sweetest milk and sugar first
I it at my own fingers nursed;
And as it grew, so every day
It waxed[1] more white and sweet than they.

It had so sweet a breath! and oft
I blushed to see its foot more soft
And white, — shall I say? — than my hand;
Nay, any lady's of the land.

It is a wondrous thing how fleet
'Twas on those little silver feet,
With what a pretty skipping grace
It oft would challenge[2] me the race!

---

[1] *waxed*, grew.   [2] *challenge*, invite (to run a race).

And when't[1] had left me far away
'Twould stay, and run again, and stay;
For it was nimbler much than hinds,[2]
And trod as if on the four winds.

I have a garden of my own,
But so with roses overgrown,
And lilies, that you would it guess
To be a little wilderness:
And all the spring-time of the year
It lovéd only to be there.

Among the beds of lilies I
Have sought it oft, where it should[3] lie,
Yet could not, till itself would rise,
Find it, although before mine eyes;
For in the flaxen lilies' shade
It like a bank of lilies laid.[4]

Upon the roses it would feed
.   Until its lips e'en seemed to bleed,
And then to me 'twould boldly trip,
And print those roses on my lip.

But all its chief delight was still
On roses thus itself to fill,
And its pure, dainty limbs to fold
In whitest sheets of lilies cold:
Had it lived long, it would have been
Lilies without — roses within.

A. MARVELL.

---

[1] *when't*, when it.   [2] *hinds*, female deer.   [3] *should*, might.
[4] *laid*, used here for 'lay,' past tense of 'lie.'

* 23 *

A NIGHT WITH A WOLF.

LITTLE one, come to my knee!
Hark, how the rain is pouring
Over the roof, in the pitch-black [1] night,
And the wind in the woods a-roaring!

Hush, my darling, and listen,
Then pay for the story with kisses;
Father was lost in the pitch-black night,
In just such a storm as this is!

High up on the lonely mountains,
Where the wild men watched and waited;
Wolves in the forest, and bears in the bush,
And I on my path belated.

The rain and the night together
Came down, and the wind came after,
Bending the props of the pine-tree roof,
And snapping many a rafter.

I crept along in the darkness,
Stunned, and bruised, and blinded, —
Crept to a fir with thick-set boughs,
And a sheltering rock behind it.

---

[1] *pitch-black*, black as pitch or tar.

There, from the blowing and raining,
   Crouching, I sought to hide me:
Something rustled, two green eyes shone —
   And a wolf lay down beside me!

Little one, be not frightened:
   I and the wolf together,
Side by side, through the long, long night,
   Hid from the awful weather.

His wet fur pressed against me;
   Each of us warmed the other;
Each of us felt in the stormy dark
   That beast and man was brother.

And, when the falling forest
   No longer crashed in warning,
Each of us went from our hiding-place
   Forth in the wild wet morning.

Darling, kiss me in payment,
   Hark! how the wind is roaring!
Father's house is a better place
   When the stormy rain is pouring.

                        BAYARD TAYLOR.

. * 24 *

LANDING OF THE PILGRIM FATHERS.

THE breaking waves dashed high
   On a stern and rock-bound coast,
And the woods against a stormy sky
   Their giant branches tossed;
And the heavy night hung dark
   The hills and waters o'er,
When a band of exiles moored their bark
   On the wild New England shore.

Not as the conqueror comes,
   They, the true-hearted, came;
Not with the roll of the stirring drums,
   And the trumpet that sings of fame:
Not as the flying come,
   In silence and in fear:
They shook the depths of the desert's gloom
   With their hymns of lofty cheer.

Amidst the storm they sang;
   And the stars heard, and the sea;
And the sounding aisles of the dim woods rang
   To the Anthem of the Free.
The ocean eagle soared
   From his nest by the white wave's foam;
And the rocking pines of the forest roared, —
   This was their welcome home!

There were men with hoary hair
　　Amidst that pilgrim band:
Why had they come to wither there,
　　Away from their childhood's land?
There was woman's fearless eye,
　　Lit by her deep love's truth:
There was manhood's brow serenely high,
　　And the fiery heart of youth.

What sought they thus afar?—
　　Bright jewels of the mine?
The wealth of seas, the spoils of war?
　　—They sought a faith's pure shrine.
Ay, call it holy ground,
　　The soil where first they trod!
They have left unstained what there they found,
　　Freedom to worship God.

FELICIA HEMANS.

* 25 *

THE ROOK AND THE LARK.

"Good-night, Sir Rook," said a little Lark;
"The daylight fades, it will soon be dark;
I've bathed my wings in the sun's last ray;
I've sung my hymn to the dying day:
So now I haste to my quiet nook
In yon dewy meadow.　Good-night, Sir Rook."

---

¹ *amain*, with might, powerfully.　　² *mere*, a pool or lake.
³ *ween*, think, fancy.

" Good-night, poor Lark," said his titled friend,
With a haughty toss and a distant bend;
" I also go to my rest profound,
But not to sleep on the cold, damp ground;
The fittest place for a bird like me
Is the topmost bough of yon tall pine-tree.

" I opened my eyes at peep of day,
And saw you taking your upward way,
Dreaming your fond romantic dreams, —
An ugly speck in the sun's bright beams, —
Soaring too high to be seen or heard,
And said to myself, ' What a foolish bird ! '

" I trod the park with a princely air;
I filled my crop with the richest fare;
I cawed all day mid a lordly crew,
And I made more noise in the world than you;
The sun shone full on my coal-black wing;
I looked and wondered. — Good-night, poor thing !"

" Good-night, once more," said the Lark's sweet
       voice;
" I see no cause to repent my choice.
You build your nest in the lofty pine;
But is your slumber more soft than mine?
You make more noise in the world than I;
But whose is the sweeter minstrelsy ?" [1]

---

[1] *minstrelsy*, music, singing, or songs.

* 26 *

TO THE LAND OF GOLD.

FAR away, where the tempests play,
  Over the lonely seas,
Sail we still, with a steady will,
  Onward before the breeze.

Onward yet, till our hearts forget
  The loves that we leave behind,
Till the memories dear that thrill in our ear
  Flow past like the whistling wind.

Let them come, — sweet thoughts of home,
  And voices we loved of old:
What care we, that sail the sea,
  Bound for a Land of Gold?

Gems there are which are lovelier far
  Than the flash of a maiden's eyes;
Jewels bright as the magic light
  That purples the evening skies.

Crowns that gleam like a fairy dream,
  Treasures of price untold;
And we are bound for that charméd ground;
  We sail for the Land of Gold!

                                W. E. LITTLEWOOD.

* 27 *

LUCY GRAY.

OFT I had heard of Lucy Gray ;
  And, when I crossed the wild,
I chanced to see at break of day
  The solitary Child.

No mate, no comrade, Lucy knew ;
  She dwelt on a wide moor, —
The sweetest thing that ever grew
  Beside a human door !

You yet may spy the fawn at play,
  The hare upon the green ;
But the sweet face of Lucy Gray
  Will never more be seen.

" To-night will be a stormy night —
  You to the town must go :
And take a lantern, child, to light
  Your mother through the snow."

" That, father, will I gladly do :
  'Tis scarcely afternoon —
The minster [1] clock has just struck two ;
  And yonder is the moon."

---

[1] *minster*, church.

At this the father raised his hook,
   And snapped a fagot band; .
He plied his work; — and Lucy took
   The lantern in her hand.

Not blither is the mountain roe:
   With many a wanton stroke
Her feet disperse the powdery snow,
   That rises up like smoke.

The storm came on before its time:
   She wandered up and down;
And many a hill did Lucy climb,
   But never reached the town.

The wretched parents all that night
   Went shouting far and wide;
But there was neither sound nor sight
   To serve them for a guide.

At daybreak on a hill they stood
   That overlooked the moor;
And thence they saw the bridge of wood,
   A furlong from their door.

They wept — and, turning homeward, cried,
   "In Heaven we all shall meet!" —
When in the snow the mother spied
   The print of Lucy's feet.

Half breathless, from the steep hill's edge
   They tracked the footmarks small;

And through the broken hawthorn hedge,
And by the long stone wall;

And then an open field they crossed —
The marks were still the same;
They tracked them on, nor ever lost;
And to the bridge they came.

They followed from the snowy bank
Those footmarks, one by one,
Into the middle of the plank —
And further there were none!

Yet some maintain that to this day
She is a living child;
That you may see sweet Lucy Gray
Upon the lonesome wild.

O'er rough and smooth she trips along
And never looks behind;
And sings a solitary song
That whistles in the wind.

W. WORDSWORTH.

* 28 *

A FAREWELL.

FLOW down, cold rivulet, to the sea,
Thy tribute wave deliver:
No more by thee my steps shall be,
Forever and forever.

Flow, softly flow, by lawn and lea,
    A rivulet, then a river:
Nowhere by thee my steps shall be,
    Forever and forever.

But here will sigh thine alder-tree,
    And here thine aspen shiver;
And here by thee will hum the bee,
    Forever and forever.

A thousand suns will stream on thee,
    A thousand moons will quiver;
But not by thee my steps shall be,
    Forever and forever.

ALFRED TENNYSON.

* 29 *

THE NORTHERN LIGHTS.

To claim the Arctic came the sun,
With banners of the burning zone, —
Unrolled upon their airy spars,
They froze beneath the light of stars;
And there they float, those streamers old,
Those Northern Lights, forever cold.

B. F. TAYLOR.

* 30 *

THE EXAMPLE OF BIRDS.

RING-DOVE, resting benignly calm,
Tell my bosom thy secret balm.
Blackbird, straining thy tuneful throat,
Teach my spirit thy thankful note.
Small wren, building thy happy nest,
Where shall I find a home of rest?
Eagle, cleaving the vaulted sky,
Teach my nature to soar on high.
Skylark, winging thy way to heaven,
Be thy track to my footsteps given!

* 31 *

SPRING.

THE Time hath laid his mantle by
Of wind and rain and icy chill,
And dons [1] a rich embroidery
Of sunlight poured on lake and hill.
No beast or bird in earth or sky,
Whose voice doth not with gladness thrill;
For Time hath laid his mantle by
Of wind and rain and icy chill.
River and fountain, brook and rill,

---

[1] *dons*, puts on, literally 'does on,' the opposite of *doffs*, 'does off.'

Bespangled o'er with livery [1] gay
Of silver droplets,[2] wind their way :
All in their new apparel vie,
For Time hath laid his mantle by.

CHARLES OF ORLEANS (1391-1465).
(*Written while a prisoner in England.*)

* 32 *

COMMON THINGS.

THE sunshine is a glorious thing
That comes alike to all,
Lighting the peasant's [3] lowly cot,
The noble's painted hall.

The moonlight is a gentle thing;
It through the window gleams
Upon the snowy pillow, where
The happy infant dreams.

It shines upon the fisher's boat
Out on the lonely sea,
Or where the little lambkins lie
Beneath the old oak-tree.

The dewdrops, on the summer morn
Sparkle upon the grass;
The village children brush them off
As through the fields they pass.

---

[1] *livery*, a kind of dress or garb.   [2] *droplets*, little drops.
[3] *peasant*, a farm-laborer in England and other countries of the Old World.

There are no gems in monarchs' crowns
  More beautiful than they,
And yet we scarcely notice them,
  But tread them off in play.

Poor robin in the pear-tree sings,
  Beside the cottage door;
The heath-flower fills the air with sweets,
  Upon the pathless moor.[1]

There are as many lovely things,
  As many pleasant tones,
For those who sit by cottage hearths
  As those who sit on thrones.

MRS. HAWKESWORTH.

* 33 *

HYMN TO THE SEASONS.

WHEN spring unlocks the flowers to paint the
  laughing soil,
When summer's balmy showers refresh the mow-
  er's toil,
When winter binds in frosty chains the fallow[2]
  and the flood,
In God the earth rejoiceth still, and owns its
  maker good.

---

[1] *moor*, an extensive tract of waste land covered with patches of heath.
[2] *fallow*, land ploughed but unsown.

The birds that wake the morning and those that
    love the shade,
The winds that sweep the mountain or lull the
    drowsy glade,
The sun that from his amber bower rejoiceth on
    his way,
The moon and stars, their Maker's name in silent
    pomp display.

Shall man, the lord of Nature, expectant of the
    sky, —
Shall man, alone unthankful, his little praise
    deny?
No: let the Year forsake his course, the Seasons
    cease to be,
Thee, Master, must we always love, and, Saviour,
    honor thee.

The flowers of spring may wither, the hope of
    summer fade,
The autumn droop in winter, the birds forsake the
    shade,
The wind be lulled, the sun and moon forget their
    old decree,[1]
But we in Nature's latest hour, O Lord! will cling
    to thee.

                        REGINALD HEBER.

See Genesis i. 16.

* 34 *

SNOW FALLING.

THE wonderful snow is falling
    Over river and woodland and wold;[1]
The trees bear spectral[2] blossoms
    In the moonshine blurred and cold.

There's a beautiful garden in heaven;
    And these are the banished flowers,
Falling and driven, and drifted
    Into this dark world of ours.

J. J. PIATT.

* 35 *

THE RAINBOW.

A FRAGMENT of a rainbow bright
    Through the moist air I see,
All dark and damp on yonder height,
    All bright and clear to me.

An hour ago the storm was here,
    The gleam was far behind:
So will our joys and griefs appear,
    When earth has ceased to blind.

Grief will be joy, if on its edge
    Fall soft that holiest ray;
Joy will be grief, if no faint pledge
    Be there of heavenly day.

J. KEBLE.

---

[1] *wold*, an open country.   [2] *spectral*, ghostly, unreal.

* 36 *

LITTLE SORROW.

AMONG the thistles on the hill,
In tears, sat Little Sorrow:
"I see a black cloud in the west,
'Twill bring a storm to-morrow;
And, when it storms, where shall I be?
And what will keep the rain from me?
Woe's me!" said Little Sorrow.

"But now the air is soft and sweet,
The sunshine bright," said Pleasure:
"Here is my pipe,[1] if you will dance,
I'll make my merriest measure;
Or, if you choose, we'll sit beneath
The red-rose tree, and twine a wreath:
Come, come with me!" said Pleasure.

"Oh, I want neither dance nor flowers;
They're not for me," said Sorrow,
"When that black cloud is in the west,
And it will storm to-morrow!
And, if it storm, what shall I do?
I have no heart to play with you:
Go, go!" said Little Sorrow.

[1] *pipe*, a kind of flute.

But lo! when came the morrow's morn,
The clouds were all blown over;
The lark sprang singing from his nest
Among the dewy clover;
And Pleasure called, "Come out and dance!
To-day you mourn no evil chance:
The clouds have all blown over!"

"But if they have, alas, alas!
Poor comfort that!" said Sorrow;
"For if to-day we miss the storm
'Twill surely come to-morrow,
And be the fiercer for delay: ·
I am too sore at heart to play.
Woe's me!" said Little Sorrow.

ANNIE D. GREEN
(MARIAN DOUGLAS).

* 37 *

LUCK AND LABOR.

LUCK doth wait, standing idly at the gate,
    Wishing, wishing, all the day;
And at night, without a fire, without a light,
    And before an empty tray,
        Doth sadly say,
" To-morrow something may turn up;
To-night on wishes I must sup."

LABOR goes, ploughing deep the fertile rows,
   Singing, singing, all the day,
And at night, before the fire, beside the light,
   And with a well-filled tray,
      Doth gladly say,
"To-morrow I'll turn something up;
To-night on wages earned I sup."

MRS. CAROLINE A. SOULE.
(In "*St. Nicholas.*")

* 38 *

PERSEVERANCE.

A SWALLOW in the spring
Came to our granary, and 'neath the eaves
Essayed[1] to make a nest, and there did bring
   Wet earth and straw and leaves.

   Day after day she toiled
With patient heart; but ere her work was crowned,
Some sad mishap the tiny fabric spoiled,
   And dashed it to the ground.

   She found the ruin wrought;[2]
But not cast down, forth from the place she flew,
And with her mate fresh earth and grasses brought,
   And built her nest anew.

---

[1] *essayed*, tried.   [2] *wrought*, worked, done.

But scarcely had she placed
The last soft feather on its ample floor,
When wicked hands, or chance, again laid waste,
And wrought the ruin o'er.

But still her heart she kept,
And toiled again ; and last night, hearing calls,
I looked, and, lo ! three little swallows slept
Within the earth-made walls.

What truth is here, O Man !
Hath hope been smitten in its early dawn ?
Have clouds o'ercast thy purpose, trust, or plan ?
— Have faith, and struggle on.

R. S. S. ANDROS

* 39 *

DISCONTENT.

Down in a field, one day in June,
    The flowers all bloomed together,
Save one, who tried to hide herself,
    And drooped, that pleasant weather.

A Robin who had flown too high,
    And felt a little lazy,
Was resting near this Buttercup
    Who wished she were a Daisy ;

For Daisies grow so trig and tall!
  She always had a passion
For wearing frills around her neck,
  In just the Daisies' fashion.

And Buttercups must always be
  The same old tiresome color;
While Daisies dress in gold and white,
  Although their gold is duller.

"Dear Robin," said this sad young flower,
  " Perhaps you'd not mind trying
To find a nice white frill for me,
  Some day when you are flying? "

"You silly thing!" the Robin said,
  "I think you must be crazy:
I'd rather be my honest self
  Than any made-up Daisy.

"You're nicer in your own bright gown;
  The little children love you:
Be the best Buttercup you can,
  And think no flower above you.

"Though Swallows leave me out of sight,
  We'd better keep our places:
Perhaps the world would all go wrong
  With one too many Daisies.

"Look bravely up into the sky,
And be content with knowing
That God wished for a Buttercup
Just here, where you are growing."

SARAH O. JEWETT.

* 40 *

THE DEWDROP AND THE STREAM.

THE brakes[1] with golden flowers were crowned,
And melody was heard around,
When, near the scene, a dewdrop shed
Its lustre on a violet's head,
And trembling to the breeze it hung.
The streamlet, as it rolled along,
The beauty of the morn confessed,
And thus the sparkling pearl addressed:

"Sure, little drop, rejoice we may,
For all is beautiful and gay;
Creation wears her emerald[2] dress,
And smiles in all her loveliness;
And with delight and pride I see
That little flower bedewed by thee:
Thy lustre with a gem might vie,
While trembling in its purple eye."

"Ay, you may well rejoice, 'tis true,"
Replied the radiant drop of dew:

---

[1] *brake*, a tract of land overgrown with ferns, furze, &c.
[2] *emerald*, green, like the precious stone of that name.

"You will, no doubt, as on you move
To flocks and herds a blessing prove.
But when the sun ascends on high,
Its beams will draw me towards the sky,
And I must own my little power —
I've but refreshed a humble flower."

"Hold!" cried the stream, "nor thus repine;
For well 'tis known a Power divine,
Subservient[1] to His will supreme,
Has made the dewdrop and the stream.
Though small thou art (I that allow),
No mark of Heaven's contempt art thou
Thou hast refreshed a humble flower,
And done according to thy power."

All things that are, both great and small,
One glorious Author formed them all:
This thought may all repinings quell, —
What serves his purpose serves him well.

* 41 *

GLAD AS A BIRD.

ALL soft and brown the upturned fields
    Lie mellow in the sun;
The very skies yield auguries[2]
    Of better days begun, —

---

[1] *subservient*, serving to promote, submissive.
[2] *yield auguries*, give out signs.

A warmth, a fulness, brooding there,
  Which nothing else could bring,
A sense of blessing in the air,
  The promise of the spring.

And shall the days of cloud and cold
  In truth no more be seen?
The snowdrop through the loosened mould
  Sends up its spikes of green;
Fresh gold upon the willow falls;
  Soft lights the uplands steep,[1]—
A strange, sweet change, whose coming calls
  Such loveliness from sleep.

And I am glad as any bird;
  It is a joy to be;[2]
There is no sound of life fresh-stirred
  But brings delight to me.
The flow of brooks, the cock's clear call
  From distant hamlets borne, —
My pulse beats happy time with all'
  These voices of the morn.

O Nature! thou my first, best friend,
  My earliest love, and best,
With us was never any end
  Of confidence and rest:

---

[1] *steep*, bathe, *i.e.*, soft lights cover the uplands.
[2] *be*, to have life.

Gayly arrayed in my yellow and green,
  When to their view I have risen,
Will they not wonder how one so serene [1]
  Came from so dismal a prison?

Many, perhaps, from so simple a flower
  This useful lesson may borrow, —
Patient to-day through its gloomiest hour,
  We come out the brighter to-morrow!

H. F. GOULD.

* 44 *

THE BEST WEALTH.

I NEITHER toil nor pray for wealth,
No riches covet, only health, —
The healthy heart, the healthy hand,
And healthy brain to understand.

With these, what need of wealth have I?
The world is mine, — earth, sea, and sky;
And every star and every flower
To give me pleasure has the power.

The meanest object I behold
Has teachings rich and manifold,
Can cheer the heart, the spirits raise,
And touch the chords of song and praise.

----

[1] *serene*, calm, unruffled.

The sun, the moon, each lucent[1] star,
The birds, the streams, my poets are:
What other pictures need I see
Than God the artist paints for me?

* 45 *

THE VIOLET.

Down in a green and shady bed
  A modest Violet grew;
Its stalk was bent, it hung its head,
  As if to hide from view.

And yet it was a lovely flower,
  Its colors bright and fair;
It might have graced a rosy bower,
  Instead of hiding there.

Yet there it was content to bloom,
  In modest tints arrayed;
And there it spread its sweet perfume
  Within the silent shade.

Then let me to the valley go
  This pretty flower to see,
That I may also learn to grow
  In sweet humility.[2]

JANE TAYLOR.

---

[1] *lucent,* shining. [2] *humility,* humbleness, lowliness.

* 46 *

TRUST IN GOD, AND DO THE RIGHT.

COURAGE, brother! do not stumble,
　Though thy path be dark as night;
There's a star to guide the humble:
　Trust in God, and do the right.

Though the road be long and dreary,
　And the goal be out of sight,
Foot it bravely, strong or weary:
　Trust in God, and do the right.

Perish, policy[1] and cunning,
　Perish, all that fears the light:
Whether losing, whether winning,
　Trust in God, and do the right.

Fly all forms of guilty passion;
　Fiends can look like angels bright;
Heed no custom, school, or fashion:
　Trust in God, and do the right.

Some will hate thee, some will love thee,
　Some will flatter, some will slight;
Cease from Man, and look above thee:
　Trust in God, and do the right.

---

[1] *policy*, art in management.

Simple rule and surest guiding,
  Inward peace and shining light;
Star upon our path abiding,
  Trust in God, and do the right.
NORMAN MACLEOD.

* 47 *

SPEAK GENTLY.

SPEAK gently; it is better far
  To rule by love than fear;
Speak gently, let no harsh words mar
  The good we might do here.

Speak gently; love doth whisper low
  The vows that true hearts bind;
And gently friendship's accents flow;
  Affection's voice is kind. .

Speak gently to the young, for they
  Will have enough to bear;
Pass through this life as best they may,
  'Tis full of anxious care.

Speak gently to the aged one;
  Grieve not the careworn heart;
The sands of life are nearly run;
  Let such in peace depart.

Speak gently, kindly, to the poor ;
  Let no harsh tone be heard ;
They have enough they must endure,
  Without an unkind word.

Speak gently to the erring ; know
  They must have toiled in vain ;
Perchance unkindness made them so :
  Oh, win them back again !

Speak gently ; 'tis a little thing
  Dropped in the heart's deep well :
The good, the joy which it may bring,
  Eternity shall tell.

* 48 *

OUR DAILY BREAD.

THE raven builds her nest on high,
  The loud winds rock her craving brood ;
The forest echoes to their cry :
  Who gives the ravens food ?

The lion goeth forth to roam
  Wild sandy hills and plains among ;
He leaves his little whelps at home :
  Who feeds the lion's young ?

God hears the hungry lion's howl;
  He feeds the ravens hoarse and gray:
Cares he alone for beast and fowl?
  Are we less dear than they?

Nay, Christian child, kneel down, and own
  The hand that feeds thee day by day;
Nor careless, with thy lip alone, —
  For "all things needful" pray.

God gave to thee thy home so dear;
  Gave store enough for frugal fare:
If richer homes have better cheer,
  'Twas God who sent it there.

But better far than garners stored,
  Than bread that honest toil may win,
Than blessings of the laden board, —
  The food he gives within.

The lion and the raven die;
  They only ask life's common bread:
Our souls shall live eternally,
  And they, too, must be fed.

Then not alone for earthly food
  Teach us with lisping tongue to pray:
The heavenly meat that makes us good,
  Lord, give us day by day.

* 49 *

THE LOST LOVE.

SHE dwelt among the untrodden ways
   Beside the springs of Dove,[1]
A maid whom there were none to praise,
   And very few to love :

A violet by a mossy stone,
   Half hidden from the eye!
Fair as a star, when only one
   Is shining in the sky.

She lived unknown, and few could know
   When Lucy ceased to be ;
But she is in her grave, and, oh
   The difference to me !

              W. WORDSWORTH.

* 50 *

HOW THE GATES CAME AJAR.

I.

'TWAS whispered one morning in heaven
   How the little child-angel May,
In the shade of the great white portal,[2]
   Sat sorrowing night and day ;

---

[1] *Dove*, a river of England, which empties into the Trent.
[2] *portal*, passage-way.

How she said to the stately warden,[1]
 He of the key and bar,
" O angel, sweet angel, I pray you,
 Set the beautiful gates ajar !

" I can hear my mother weeping ;
 She is lonely, she cannot see
A glimmer of light in the darkness,.
 Where the gates shut after me.
Oh ! turn me the key, sweet angel,
 The splendor will shine so far ! "
But the warden answered, " I dare not
 Set the beautiful gates ajar."

II.

Then rose up Mary the blessed,
 Sweet Mary, mother of Christ ;
Her hand on the hand of the angel
 She laid, and her touch sufficed :
Turned was the key in the portal,
 Fell ringing the golden bar ;
And lo ! in the little child's fingers
 Stood the beautiful gates ajar.

" And this key, for further using
 To my blessed Son shall be given,"
Said Mary, mother of Jesus,
 Tenderest heart in heaven.
Now, never a sad-eyed mother

---

[1] *warden*, one who keeps guard or ward.

But may catch the glory afar,
Since safe in the Lord Christ's bosom
Are the keys of the gates ajar, —
Close hid in the dear Christ's bosom,
And the gates forever ajar !

* 51 *

SOWING.

ARE we sowing the seeds of kindness?
They shall blossom bright ere long;
Are we sowing the seeds of discord?[1]
They shall ripen into wrong;
Are we sowing seeds of honor?
They shall bring forth golden grain;
Are we sowing seeds of falsehood?
We shall yet reap bitter pain:
— Whatso'er our sowing be,
Reaping, we its fruits shall see.

We can never be too careful
What the seed our hands shall sow;
Love from love is sure to ripen;
Hate from hate is sure to grow.
Seeds of good or ill we scatter
Heedlessly along our way;
But a glad or grievous fruitage[2]
Waits us at the harvest day.
— Whatso'er our sowing be,
Reaping, we its fruits must see.

---

[1] *discord,* strife.　　　[2] *fruitage,* fruit collectively.

* 52 *

SEEDS AND FRUITS.

WE scatter seeds with careless hand,
  And dream we ne'er shall see them more ;
    But for a thousand years
    Their fruit appears
  In seeds that mar the land,
    Or healthful store !

The deeds we do, the words we say,
  Into still air they seem to fleet ;
    We count them ever past ;
    But they shall last :
  In the dread Judgment they
    And we shall meet.

J. KEBLE.

* 53 *

THE BETTER LAND.

"I HEAR thee speak of the Better Land ;
Thou call'st its children a happy band ;
Mother, oh, where is that radiant shore ?
Shall we not seek it, and weep no more ?
Is it where the flower of the orange blows,
And the fire-flies glance through the myrtle
    boughs ? "
"Not there, not there, my child ! "

" Is it where the feathery palm-trees rise,
And the date grows ripe under sunny skies?
Or midst the green islands of glittering seas,
Where fragrant forests perfume the breeze,
And strange bright birds on their starry wings
Bear the rich hues of all glorious things?"
  " Not there, not there, my child."

" Is it far away in some region old,
Where the rivers wander o'er sands of gold,
Where the burning rays of the ruby shine,
And the diamond lights up the secret mine,
And the pearl gleams forth from the coral strand?
Is it there, dear mother, — that Better Land?"
  " Not there, not there, my child.

" Eye hath not seen it, my gentle boy;
Ear hath not heard its deep songs of joy;
Dreams cannot picture a world so fair;
Sorrow and Death may not enter there;
Time does not breathe on its fadeless bloom,
For beyond the clouds, and beyond the tomb,
  It is there, it is there, my child!"
    FELICIA HEMANS.

* 54 *

SUMMER MOODS.

I LOVE at eventide [1] to walk alone
Down narrow glens o'erhung with dewy thorn,
Where, from the long grass underneath, the snail,
Jet black, creeps out and sprouts his timid horn.
I love to muse o'er meadows newly mown,
Where withering grass perfumes the sultry air,
Where bees search round, with sad and weary
    drone,
In vain, for flowers that bloomed but newly there;
While in the juicy corn the hidden quail
Cries " Wet my foot; " and, hid as thoughts un-
    born,
The fairy-like and seldom seen land-rail [2]
Utters, " Craik, craik ! " like voices underground,
Right glad to meet the evening's dewy veil,
And see the light fade into gloom around.

J. CLARE.

* 55 *

THE DAFFODILS.

I WANDERED lonely as a cloud
    That floats on high o'er vales and hills,
When all at once I saw a crowd,
    A host of golden daffodils,
Beside the lake, beneath the trees,
Fluttering and dancing in the breeze.

---

[1] *eventide*, evening (' tide' originally meant ' time ').
[2] *land-rail*, also called the *corn-crake*, is allied to the snipe.

Continuous [1] as the stars that shine
And twinkle on the milky way,
They stretched in never-ending line
Along the margin [2] of a bay :
Ten thousand saw I at a glance,
Tossing their heads in sprightly dance.

The waves beside them danced, but they
Outdid the sparkling waves in glee : —
A poet could not but be gay
In such a jocund company.
I gazed, and gazed, but little thought
What wealth [3] the show to me had brought:

For oft, when on my couch I lie
In vacant or in pensive mood, [4]
They flash upon that inward eye [5]
Which is the bliss of solitude;
And then my heart with pleasure fills,
And dances with the daffodils.

W. WORDSWORTH.

* 56 *

THE CREATION.

ALL things bright and beautiful,
All creatures great and small,
All things wise and wonderful,
The Lord God made them all.

---

[1] *continuous*, close together.   [3] *wealth*, benefit.
[2] *margin*, edge.   [4] idle or thoughtful.
[5] *inward eye*, thought.   ‧

Each little flower that opens,
Each little bird that sings,
He made their glowing colors,
He made their tiny wings.

The rich man in his castle,
The poor man at his gate,
God made them, high or lowly,
And ordered their estate.[1]

The purple-headed [2] mountain,
The river running by,
The sunset, and the morning
That brightens up the sky,

The cold wind in the winter,
The pleasant summer sun,
The ripe fruits in the garden, —
He made them every one.

The tall trees in the greenwood,
The meadows where we play,
The rushes by the water
We gather every day, —

He gave us eyes to see them,
And lips that we might tell
How great is God Almighty
Who has made all things well.

C. F. ALEXANDER.

[1] *estate*, condition in life, rank.
[2] *purple-headed*, the top of a purple color, because of the distance.

* 58 *

THE SWEET SONG OF SONGS.

THE leaf-tongues of the forest, the flower-lips of
the sod,
The happy birds that hymn their rapture in the
ear of God,
The summer wind that bringeth music over land
and sea,
Have each a voice that singeth this sweet song of
songs to me : —
" This world is full of beauty, like other worlds
above,
And if we did our duty it might be full of
love."

G. MASSEY.

* 59 *

SONG OF LIFE.

A TRAVELLER through a dusty road
Strewed acorns on the lea,
And one took root and sprouted up
And grew into a tree.

Love sought its shade at even-time
To breathe its early vows,
And Age was pleased, in heats of noon,
To bask beneath its boughs :

The dormouse loved its dangling twigs,
  The birds sweet music bore :
It stood a glory in its place, —
  A blessing evermore !

A little spring had lost its way
  Amid the grass and fern ;
A passing stranger scooped a well
  Where weary men might turn.

He walled it in, and hung with care
  A ladle at the brink ;
He thought not of the deed he did,
  But judged that Toil might drink.

He passed again, and lo ! the well,
  By summers never dried,
Had cooled ten thousand parchéd tongues,
  And saved a life beside.

A dreamer dropped a random thought ;
  'Twas old, and yet was new —
A simple fancy of the brain,
  But strong in being true ;

It shone upon a genial mind,
  And lo ! its light became
A lamp of life, a beacon ray,
  A monitory flame.

The thought was small — its issue great :
  A watch-fire on the hill,

It sheds its radiance far adown,
　And cheers the valley still!

A nameless man, amid a crowd
　That thronged the daily mart
Let fall a word of Hope and Love
Unstudied from the heart—

　A whisper on the tumult thrown,
　　A transitory breath, —
　It raised a brother from the dust,
　　It saved a soul from death.

　O germ! O fount! O word of love!
　　O thought at random [1] cast!
　Ye were but little at the first,
　　But mighty at the last.

C. MACKAY.

* 60 *

GOOD LIFE, LONG LIFE.

HE liveth long who liveth well;
　All else is life but flung away:
He liveth longest who can tell
　Of true things truly done each day.

Then fill each hour with what will last;
　Buy up the moments as they go:
The life above, when this is past,
　Is the ripe fruit of life below.

---

　[1] *at random*, without any aim or purpose.

Sow love, and taste its fruitage pure,
  Sow peace, and reap its harvest bright,
Sow sunbeams on the rock and moor,
  And find a harvest-home of light.

                                    H. BONAR.

* 61 *

THE NOBLE NATURE.

IT is not growing like a tree
In bulk doth make men better be;
Or standing long an oak, three hundred year,
To fall a log at last, dry, bald, and sear :[1]
      A lily of a day
      Is fairer far in May,
Although it fall and die that night, —
It was the plant and flower of Light :
In small proportions we just beauties see,
And in short measures life may perfect be.

                                    BEN JONSON.

* 62 *

OUR STATE.

THE South land boasts its teeming cane;
The prairied West, its heavy grain ;
And sunset's radiant gates unfold
On rising marts and sands of gold.

---

[1] *sear*, withered.

Rough, bleak, and hard, our little State
Is scant of soil, of limits strait;[1]
Her yellow sands are sands alone,
Her only mines are ice and stone.

From autumn frost to April rain,
Too long her winter woods complain;
From budding flower to falling leaf,
Her summer time is all too brief.

Yet on her rocks and on her sands
And wintry hills the schoolhouse stands;
And what her rugged soil denies
The harvest of the mind supplies.

The riches of the Commonwealth[2]
Are free strong minds and hearts of health;
And, more to her than gold or grain,
The cunning hand and cultured brain.

For well she keeps her ancient stock, —
The stubborn strength of Pilgrim Rock;
And still maintains with milder laws
And clearer light, the Good Old Cause!

Nor heeds the sceptic's puny hands,
While near her school the church-spire stands;
Nor fears the blinded bigot's rule,
While near her church-spire stands the school.

J. G. WHITTIER.

---

[1] *strait*, limited.   [2] *Commonwealth*, the State.

* 63 *

ABOU BEN ADHEM AND THE ANGEL.

ABOU BEN ADHEM (may his tribe incrèase !)
Awoke one night from a deep dream of peace,
And saw, within the moonlight in his room,
Making it rich, and like a lily in bloom,
An Angel writing in a book of gold.

Exceeding peace had made Ben Adhem bold,
And to the Presence in the room he said,
"What writest thou?" The Vision raised its
    head,
And with a look made of all sweet[1] accord[2]
Answered, "The names of those who love the
    Lord."

"And is mine one?" said Abou. "Nay, not so,"
Replied the Angel. Abou spoke more low,
But cheerly still, and said, "I pray thee, then,
Write me as one that loves his fellow men."

The Angel wrote and vanished. The next night
It came again with a great wakening light,
And showed the names whom love of God had
    blessed,
And, lo! Ben Adhem's name led all the rest.

                                    LEIGH HUNT.

[1] *all sweet*, wholly or very sweet.   [2] *accord*, harmony.

* 64 *

THE THRUSH'S NEST.

WITHIN a thick and spreading hawthorn bush
　That overhung a mole-hill large and round,
I heard from morn to morn a merry thrush
　Sing hymns of rapture, while I drank the sound
With joy; and oft, an unintruding guest,
　I watched her secret toils from day to day,
How true she warped the moss to form her nest,
　And modelled it within with wool and clay.

And by and by, like heath-bells gilt with dew,
　There lay her shining eggs as bright as flowers,
Ink-spotted over, shells of green and blue;
　And there I witnessed in the summer hours
A brood of Nature's minstrels chirp and fly,
　Glad as the sunshine and the laughing sky.

J. CLARE.

* 65 *

THE BIRD IN A CAGE.

OH! who would keep a little bird confined,
When cowslip [1] bells are nodding in the wind,
When every hedge as with "good-morrow" rings,
And heard from wood to wood the blackbird
　　sings?

---

[1] *cowslip*, the English cowslip, — a species of primrose.

Oh! who would keep a little bird confined
In his cold wiry prison ?   Let him fly,
And hear him sing, " How sweet is Liberty!"
W. L. Bowles.

* 66 *

THE WORM.

Turn, turn, thy hasty foot aside,
  Nor crush that helpless worm!
The frame thy wayward [1] looks deride
  Required a God to form.

The common Lord of all that move,
  From whom thy being flowed,
A portion of his boundless love
  On that poor worm bestowed.

The sun, the moon, the stars, he made
  For all his creatures free,
And spread o'er earth the grassy blade,
  For worms, as well as thee.

Let them enjoy their little day,
  Their humble bliss receive ;
Oh! do not lightly take away
  The life thou canst not give.
– T. Gisborne.

---

[1] *wayward*, wilful.

* 67 *

THE NIGHTINGALE AND THE GLOW-WORM.

A NIGHTINGALE, that all day long
Had cheered the village with his song,
Nor yet at eve his note suspended,
Nor yet when eventide was ended,
Began to feel, as well he might,
The keen demands of appetite ;
When, looking eagerly around,
He spied far off, upon the ground,
A something shining in the dark,
And knew the Glowworm by his spark:
So, stooping down from hawthorn top,
He thought to put him in his crop.
The worm, aware of his intent,
Harangued him thus, right eloquent:
"Did you admire my lamp," quoth he,
" As much as I your minstrelsy,
You would abhor to do me wrong,
As much as I to spoil your song ;
For 'twas the self-same Power Divine
Taught you to sing and me to shine,
That you with music, I with light,
Might beautify and cheer the night."
The songster heard this short oration,
And, warbling out his approbation,
Released him, as my story tells,
And found a supper somewhere else.

W. COWPER.

⁎ * 68 *

BEAUTIFUL THINGS.

WHAT millions of beautiful things there must be
In this mighty world! Who could reckon them
    all? —
The tossing, the foaming, the wide flowing sea,
And thousands of rivers that into it fall.

Oh, there are the mountains, half covered with
    snow;
And tall and dark trees, like a girdle of green;
And waters that wind in the valleys below,
Or roar in the caverns, too deep to be seen.

Vast caves in the earth, full of wonderful things,
The bones of strange animals, jewels, and spars;[1]
Or, far up in Iceland, the hot boiling springs,
Like fountains of feathers or showers of stars!

Here spread the sweet meadows with thousands of
    flowers;
Far away are old woods that for ages have grown:
Wild elephants sleep in the shade of their bowers,
Or troops of young antelopes think them their own.

Oh, yes, they are glorious all to behold,
And pleasant to read of, and curious to know;
And something of God and his wisdom we're told,
Whatever we look at, wherever we go.

                       JANE TAYLOR.

[1] *spar*, a shining mineral.

* 69 * ·

LOSS OF THE ROYAL GEORGE.

Toll for the Brave !
　The brave that are no more !
All sunk beneath the wave
　Fast by [1] their native shore !

Eight hundred of the brave,
　Whose courage well was tried,
Had make the vessel heel,[2]
　And laid her on her side.

A land breeze shook the shrouds,[3]
　And she was overset ;
Down went the Royal George,
　With all her crew complete !

Toll for the brave !
　Brave Kempenfelt is gone ;
His last sea-fight is fought,
　His work of glory done.

It was not in the battle ;
　No tempest gave the shock ;
She sprang no fatal leak ; [4]
　She ran upon no rock.

---

[1] *fast by*, near.　　[3] *shrouds*, mast-ropes.
[2] *heel*, lean over.　[4] *spring a leak*, to leak by means of a sudden breach.

His sword was in its sheath,
His fingers held the pen,
When Kempenfelt went down
With twice four hundred men.

Weigh [1] the vessel up,
Once dreaded by our foes,
And mingle with our cup [2]
The tears that England owes.

Her timbers yet are sound,
And she may float again,
Full charged with England's thunder,[3]
And plough the distant main.

But Kempenfelt is gone,
His victories are o'er;
And he and his eight hundred
Shall plough the wave no more.

W. COWPER.

The Royal George, a man-of-war carrying 108 guns, commanded by
Admiral Kempenfelt, while partially careened to have her seams calked, in
Portsmouth Harbor, England, was overset about ten A.M., Aug. 29, 1782.
The total loss was believed to be near one thousand souls.

[1] *weigh*, lift.   [2] *cup*, rejoicing.   [3] *thunder*, noise of cannon.

* 70 *

HOW THE NEW YEAR CAME.

THE sun was sinking out of sight:
  " Bessie," said Herbert, " have you heard?
  It's really true, upon my word!
This year is going away to-night!
  It's time is up, they say, and so
  At midnight it will have to go.
  And right away another year
  Will come along, a real new year,
  As soft as any mouse, —
So soft, we'll hardly hear it creep, —
  Yes, come right to this very house,
While every one's asleep! "

Now Bessie's eyes grew wide to hear.
  " Let's keep awake," she cried, "and so
  We'll see one come and see one go.
Two years at once! Won't that be queer?
  Let's tell the New Year it is bad,
  We want the one we've always had,
With birds and flowers and things, you know,
  And funny ice and pretty snow.
  It had my birthday, too, in May,
And yours — when was it? and you know
  How it had Fourth o' July one day,
And Christmas. Oh, it *mustn't* go! "

" Ha, ha ! " laughed Herbert. " What a Bess !
This year was new when first it came;
The next one will be just the same
As this that's going now, I guess.
— That's nothing. But what bothers me
Is how the change is going to be.
I can't see how one year can go
And one can come at midnight, so   .
All in a minute : *that's* the bother !
I've heard them say, 'the rolling year : '
You'd think they'd roll on one another,
Unless they knew just how to steer."

The speck of time 'twixt night and day
    Was close at hand. Herbert and Bess
    Had won their parents' smiling " yes "
To watch the old year go away.
    Nurse on the lounge found easy rest
    Till Bess should come to be undrest :
All but the children were asleep,
And years might roll, or years might creep,
For all they cared ; while Bess and Bert,
Who never stirred, and scarcely spoke,
    Watched the great clock, awake, alert,
All breathless for the coming stroke.

                                        .

Soon Bessie whispered, " Moll don't care."
    Moll was her doll. And Herbert said,
    " The clock's so far up overhead
It makes me wink to watch it there,

The great tall thing! Let's look inside."
And so its door they opened wide.
Tick-a-tick! How loud it sounded!
Bessie's heart with wonder bounded.
How the great round thing that hung
Down the middle swung and swung!
Tick, a-tick, a-tick, a-tick, —
Dear how loud it was, and quick!
Tick-a, tick-a, tick-a, tick-a!
Surely it was growing quicker!
While the swinging thing kept on,
Back and forth, and never done.

There! It's coming! Loud and clear
Each ringing stroke the night alarms.
Bess, screaming, hid in Herbert's arms.
" The year!" he cried, " the year! the year!"
" Where?" faltered Bessie, "which? where,
'bouts?"
But still " The year!" glad Herbert shouts ;
And still the steady strokes rang on
Until the banished year was gone.
" We've seen the Old Year out — hurrah!"
" Oh, oh!" sobbed Bessie, " call mamma.
I don't like years to racket so :
It frightens me to hear 'em go."
But Herbert kissed away her tears,
And, gently soothing all her fears,
He heard the New Year coming quick, —
Tick, a-tick, a-tick, a-tick.

MARY MAPES DODGE.

* 71 *

HOHENLINDEN.[1]

On Linden, when the sun was low,
All bloodless lay the untrodden snow;
And dark as winter was the flow
Of Iser,[2] rolling rapidly.

But Linden saw another sight,
When the drum beat at dead of night
Commanding fires of death to light
The darkness of her scenery.

By torch and trumpet fast arrayed,[3]
Each horseman drew his battle-blade,
And furious every charger[4] neighed,
To join the dreadful revelry.[5]

Then shook the hills with thunder riven;
Then rushed the steed, to battle driven;
And louder than the bolts of Heaven[6]
Far flashed the red artillery.[7]

---

[1] This battle, which was witnessed by the poet, was fought December 2, 1800, between the Austrians under Archduke John, and the French under Moreau, in a forest near Munich. Hohenlinden means *High Lime-trees.*

[2] *Iser* (pronounced *ē'zer*), a river on which Munich is situated.

[3] *arrayed,* drawn up in order, ready for battle.

[4] *charger,* war-horse.

[5] *revelry,* the noise and tumult of battle; *commonly,* loose and noisy festivity.

[6] than the thunder.

[7] *artillery,* cannon.

But redder yet that light shall glow
On Linden's hills of stainéd snow,
And bloodier yet the torrent flow
   Of Iser, rolling rapidly.

'T is morn; but scarce yon level sun
Can pierce the war-clouds, rolling dun,[1]
Where furious Frank and fiery Hun[2]
   Shout in their sulphurous canopy.[3]

The combat deepens. On, ye Brave
Who rush to glory, or the grave!
Wave, Munich![4] all thy banners wave,
   And charge with all thy chivalry![5]

Few, few shall part where many meet!
The snow shall be their winding-sheet;
And every turf beneath their feet
   Shall be a soldier's sepulchre.[6]

T. CAMPBELL.

[1] *dun*, black, gloomy.
[2] *Frank*, Frenchman; *Hun*, Austrian.
[3] *sulphurous canopy*, overhanging smoke from guns.
[4] *Munich* (pronounced *mu'nik*).
[5] *chivalry*, cavalry or horsemen.
[6] *sepulchre*, grave.

* 72 *

A TRAGIC STORY.

THERE lived a sage in days of yore,
And he a handsome pigtail wore,
But wondered much, and sorrowed more,
    Because it hung behind him.

He mused upon this curious case,
And vowed he'd change the pigtail's place,
And have it hanging at his face,
    Not dangling there behind him.

Says he, " The mystery I've found !
I'll turn me round." — He turned him round ;
    But still it hung behind him.

Then round and round, and out and in,
All day the puzzled sage did spin :
In vain ! it mattered not a pin !
    The pigtail hung behind him.

And right and left, and round about,
And up and down, and in and out
He turned ; but still the pigtail stout
    Hung steadily behind him.

And though his efforts never slack,
And though he twist, and twirl, and tack,
Alas ! still faithful to his back,
    The pigtail hangs behind him.

W. M. THACKERAY
(From the German of CHAMISSO).

* 73 *

THE CAMEL'S NOSE.

ONCE in his shop a workman wrought,
With languid head and listless thought,
When, through the open window's space,
Behold, a camel thrust his face!
"My nose is cold," he meekly cried;
"Oh, let me warm it by thy side!"

Since no denial word was said,
In came the nose, in came the head:
As sure as sermon follows text,
The long and scraggy neck came next;
And then, as falls the threatening storm,
In leaped the whole ungainly form.

Aghast the owner gazed around,
And on the rude invader frowned,
Convinced, as closer still he pressed,
There was no room for such a guest;
Yet more astonished, heard him say,
"If thou art troubled, go away,
For in this place I choose to stay."

O youthful hearts to gladness born,
Treat not this Arab lore with scorn!
To evil habits' earliest wile
Lend neither ear, nor glance, nor smile;
Choke the dark fountain ere it flows,
Nor e'en admit the camel's nose!

MRS. L. H. SIGOURNEY.

* 77 *

THE HEAVENS DECLARE GOD'S GLORY.

THE spacious firmament on high,
With all the blue ethereal [1] sky,
And spangled heavens, a shining frame,
Their great Original proclaim.

The unwearied sun, from day to day,
Doth his Creator's power display,
And publishes to every land
The work of an Almighty hand.

Soon as the evening shades prevail,
The moon takes up the wondrous tale,
And nightly to the listening earth
Repeats the story of her birth;

While all the stars that round her burn,
And all the planets, in their turn,
Confirm the tidings as they roll,
And spread the truth from pole to pole.

What though, in solemn silence, all
Move round this great terrestrial [2] ball?
What though no real voice nor sound
Amid their radiant orbs be found?

[1] *ethereal*, heavenly.   [2] *terrestrial*, earthly.

In Reason's ear they all rejoice,
And utter forth a glorious voice, —
Forever singing, as they shine,
" The hand that made us is divine."

JOSEPH ADDISON.

* 78 *

BUGLE SONG.

THE splendor falls on castle walls,
　　And snowy summits old in story;
The long light shakes across the lakes,
　　And the wild cataract leaps in glory.
Blow, bugle, blow, set the wild echoes flying:
Blow, bugle; answer, echoes, dying, dying, dying.

Oh hark! oh hear! how thin and clear,
　　And thinner, clearer, farther going!
Oh sweet and far from cliff and scar[1]
　　The horns of Elfland[2] faintly blowing!
Blow, let us hear the purple glens replying:
Blow, bugle; answer, echoes, dying, dying, dying.

O Love, they die in yon rich sky,
　　They faint on hill, or field, or river:
Our echoes roll from soul to soul,
　　And grow forever and forever:
Blow, bugle, blow, set the wild echoes flying,
And answer, echoes, answer, dying, dying, dying.

ALFRED TENNYSON.

[1] *scar*, a bare and broken place on the side of a mountain.
[2] *Elfland*, fairy-land.

* 79 *

ASPIRATIONS OF YOUTH.

HIGHER, higher, will we climb
  Up the mount of glory,
That our names may live through time
  In our country's story:
Happy, when her welfare calls,
He who conquers, he who falls.

Deeper, deeper, let us toil
  In the mines of knowledge,
Nature's wealth and Learning's spoil
  Win from school and college;
Delve we there for richer gems
Than the stars of diadems.

Onward, onward, may we press
  Through the path of duty;
Virtue is true happiness,
  Excellence true beauty:
Minds are of celestial birth,
Make we, then, a heaven of earth.

Closer, closer, let us knit
  Hearts and hands together,
Where our fireside comforts sit
  In the wildest weather:
Oh, they wander wide who roam
For the joys of life from home.

                JAMES MONTGOMERY.

* 80 *

GEORGE NIDIVER.

MEN have done brave deeds,
  And bards have sung them well:
I of George Nid'iver
  Now the tale will tell.

In Californian mountains,
  A hunter bold was he:
Keen his eye and sure his aim
  As any you should see.

A little Indian boy
  Followed him everywhere,
Eager to share the hunter's joy,
  The hunter's meal to share:

And when the bird or deer
  Fell by the hunter's skill,
The boy was always near
  To help with right good-will.

One day as through the cleft
  Between two mountains steep,
Shut in both right and left,
  Their questing way they keep,

They see two grizzly bears,
  With hunger fierce and fell,
Rush at them unawares,
  Right down the narrow dell.

The boy turned round with screams,
  And ran with terror wild :
One of the pair of savage beasts
  Pursued the shrieking child.

The hunter raised his gun, —   ·
  He knew *one* charge was all, —
And through the boy's pursuing foe
  He sent his only ball.

The other bear, now furious,
  Came on with dreadful pace;
The hunter stood unarmed,
  And met him-face to face.

I say *unarmed* he stood :
  Against those frightful paws,
For rifle butt or club of wood,
  Could stand no more than straws. ·

George Nidiver stood still,
  And looked him in the face ;
The wild beast stopped amazed,
  Then came with slackening pace.

Still firm the hunter stood,
  Although his heart beat high ;
Again the creature stopped,
  And gazed with wondering eye.

The hunter met his gaze,
  Nor yet an inch gave way ;

The bear turned slowly round
  And slowly moved away ·

What thoughts were in his mind
  It would be hard to spell; [1]
What thoughts were in George Nidiver's
  I rather guess than tell.

Be sure that rifle's aim,
  Swift choice of generous part,
Showed, in its passing gleam,
  The depths of a brave heart.

RALPH WALDO EMERSON.

* 81 *

HOW SLEEP THE BRAVE!

How sleep the Brave who sink to rest
By all their country's wishes blest!
When Spring, with dewy fingers cold,
Returns to deck their hallowed mould,
She there shall dress a sweeter sod
Than Fancy's feet have ever trod.

By fairy hands their knell is rung;
By forms unseen their dirge is sung;
There Honor comes, a pilgrim gray,
To bless the turf that wraps their clay;
And Freedom shall awhile repair,
To dwell a weeping hermit there!

W. COLLINS.

[1] *spell*, relate — an old use of the word.

* 82 *

THE BUILDERS.

ALL are architects of Fate,
  Working in these walls of Time;
Some with massive deeds and great,
  Some with ornaments of rhyme.

Nothing useless is, or low;
  Each thing in its place is best;
And what seems but idle show
  Strengthens and supports the rest.

For the structure that we raise,
  Time is with materials filled:
Our to-days and yesterdays
  Are the blocks with which we build.

Truly shape and fashion these;
  Leave no yawning gaps between:
Think not, because no man sees,
  Such things will remain unseen.

In the elder days of Art
  Builders wrought with greatest care
Each minute [1] and unseen part;
  For the gods see everywhere.

---

[1] *minute'*, very small or little.

Let us do our work as well,
   Both the unseen and the seen, —
Make the house, where Gods may dwell.
   Beautiful, entire, and clean.

Else our lives are incomplete,
   Standing in these walls of Time,
Broken stairways, where the feet
   Stumble as they seek to climb.

Build to-day, then, strong and sure,
   With a firm and ample base ;
And ascending and secure
   Shall to-morrow find its place.

Thus alone can we attain
   To those turrets, where the eye
Sees the world as one vast plain,
   And one boundless reach of sky.

H. W. LONGFELLOW.

* 83 *

THE NOBLY BORN.

Who counts himself as nobly born
   Is noble in despite of place ;
And honors are but brands to one
   Who wears them not with nature's grace.

The prince may sit with clown or churl,
   Nor feel himself disgraced thereby ;

But he who has but small esteem
Husbands that little carefully.

Then, be thou peasant, be thou peer,
  Count it still more thou art thine own:
Stand on a larger heraldry [1]
  Than that of nation or of zone. [2]

What though not bid to knightly halls?
  Those halls have missed a courtly guest;
That mansion is not privileged, [3]
  Which is not open to the best.

Give honor due when custom asks,
  Nor wrangle for this lesser claim;
It is not to be destitute,
  To have the thing without the name.

Then dost thou come of gentle blood,
  Disgrace not thy good company;
If lowly born, so bear thyself
  That gentle blood may come of thee.

Strive not with pain to scale the height
  Of some fair garden's petty wall,
But climb the open mountain side,
  Whose summit rises over all.

E. S. H.

---

[1] that is, be a true man, free from narrow prejudices.
[2] *zone*, a great division of the earth's surface.
[3] *privileged*, granted some benefit.

* 84 *

DIVINE CARE.

THE insect that with puny wing
  Just shoots along the summer ray,
The floweret which the breath of spring
  Wakes into life for half a day,
The smallest mote, the slenderest hair, —
All feel our common Father's care.

E'en from the glories of his throne
  He bends to view this wandering ball;
Sees all, as if that all were one;
  Loves one, as if that one were all;
Rolls the swift planets in their spheres,
And counts the sinner's lonely tears.

* 85 *

THE CORAL GROVE.

DEEP in the wave is a coral grove,
Where the purple mullet and gold-fish rove;
Where the sea-flower spreads its leaves of blue
That never are wet with falling dew,
But in bright and changeful beauty shine,
Far down in the green and glassy brine.

The floor is of sand, like the mountain drift;
And the pearl-shells spangle the flinty snow;
From coral rocks the sea-plants lift
Their boughs where the tides and billows flow.

The water is calm and still below,
For the winds and waves are absent there;
And the sands are bright as the stars that glow
In the motionless fields of upper air.

There, with its waving blade of green,
The sea-flag streams through the silent water;
And the crimson leaf of the dulse [1] is seen
To blush like a banner bathed in slaughter.
There, with a light and easy motion,
The fan-coral sweeps through the clear deep sea;
And the yellow and scarlet tufts of ocean
Are bending like corn on the upland lea;
And life, in rare and beautiful forms,
Is sporting amid those bowers of stone,
And is safe when the wrathful Spirit of storms
Has made the top of the wave his own.

And when the ship from his fury flies,
Where the myriad voices of Ocean roar;
When the wind-god frowns in the murky skies,
And demons are waiting the wreck on shore, —
Then, far below, in the peaceful sea,
The purple mullet and gold-fish rove;
While the waters murmur tranquilly
Through the bending twigs of the coral grove.

J. G. PERCIVAL.

[1] *dulse*, a sea-weed of a reddish-brown color.

* 86 *

CONTENTMENT.

WHY need I strive and sigh for wealth?
　　It is enough for me
That Heaven hath sent me strength and health,
　　A spirit glad and free:
Grateful these blessings to receive,
I sing my hymn at morn and eve.

On some what floods of riches flow!
　　House. herds, and gold have they;
Yet life's best joys they never know,
　　But fret their hours away.
The more they have, they seek increase:[1]
Complaints and cravings never cease.

A vale of gloom this world they call;
　　But. oh! I find it fair:
Much happiness it has for all,
　　And none are grudged a share.
The little birds on new-tried wing,
And insects, revel in the spring.

For love'of us. hills. woods, and plains
　　In beauteous hues are clad;
And birds sing far and near sweet strains,
　　Caught up by echoes glad.
" Rise." sings the lark. " your tasks to ply:"
The nightingale sings, " Lullaby."

---

[1] The more they have, the more they want — strive to get.

And when the obedient sun goes forth,
 And all like gold appears;
When bloom o'erspreads the glowing earth,
 And fields have ripening ears, —
I think those glories that I see
My kind Creator made for me.

Then loud I thank the Lord above,
 And say in joyful mood,
His love, it is a Father's love,
 He wills to all men good.
Then let us ever grateful live,
Enjoying all He deigns to give.

Johann Miller.

* 87 *

TRUST.

I know not if or dark or bright
 Shall be my lot;
If that wherein my hopes delight
 Be best, or not.

It may be mine to drag for years
 Toil's heavy chain;
Or day and night my meat be tears
 On bed of pain.

Dear faces may surround my hearth
 With smiles and glee;
Or I may dwell alone, and mirth
 Be strange to me.

My bark is wafted to the strand
 By breath divine;
And on the helm there rests a hand
 Other than mine.

One who has known in storms to sail
 I have on board;
Above the raving of the gale
 I hear my Lord.

He holds me when the billows smite, —
 I shall not fall.
If sharp, 'tis short; if long, 'tis light, —
 He tempers all.

Safe to the land, safe to the land, —
 The end is this,
And then with Him go hand in hand
 Far into bliss.

DEAN OF CANTERBURY.

Press of Rand, Avery, & Co.

"As interesting as Robinson Crusoe."

YOUNG FOLKS' BOOK

OF

AMERICAN EXPLORERS.

BY

THOMAS WENTWORTH HIGGINSON.

UNIFORM WITH "HIGGINSON'S YOUNG FOLKS' HISTORY OF THE UNITED STATES."

. 16mo. Cloth. Illustrated. $1.50.

"The author of this marvellously interesting book has acted on the sensible idea that accounts of the adventures and experiences of early navigators to America from Europe must be of quite as great interest as the tale of Robinson Crusoe; and taking, as he has, extracts from the veritable histories of · the ancient mariners who sought these then unknown shores, he has furnished interesting and healthful reading, which is ADMIRABLY CALCULATED TO GIVE THE YOUNG A TASTE FOR SEARCHING HISTORY. He gives some account of the early Norsemen and their discoveries, of Columbus, De Soto, Captain John Smith, and others, including Pocahontas, Miles Standish, the Pilgrims, and all prominent persons in the settlement of the colonies. The book is elegantly printed and bound, and generously illustrated." — *Pittsburg Despatch.*

"This book reminds one of Dickens's Child's History of England, and we could scarcely pay it a higher compliment. It begins with the legends about the Northmen, and goes on with Columbus, the Cabots, De Vaca, Cartier, De Soto, and so on down to Henry Hudson. THE BEAUTY OF THE MATTER IS THAT IT IS ORIGINAL, — CONSISTS OF EXTRACTS FROM THE ORIGINAL NARRATIVES OF THE EXPLORERS THEMSELVES. It is a book for every boy and girl in the land to read." — *Methodist, N.Y.*

"Colonel Higginson has searched all accessible sources for his materials, and has used them very skilfully. For young people his book is sure to have all the charm of stories of romance and adventure, while, at the same time, it conveys information not readily obtainable in so pleasant a shape elsewhere. The attractiveness of the book is increased by many excellent wood-engravings, some of them full-page. The typography and paper are of the best ; and in externals the book is uniform with Colonel Higginson's Young Folks' History of the United States, which latter volume, by the way, has found an extensive sphere of usefulness as a text-book, as well as for purposes of general reading and entertainment." — *Journal.*

Sold by all booksellers, and sent by mail, post-paid, on receipt of price.

LEE & SHEPARD, Publishers, Boston.

AIDS TO EDUCATION.

Hand-Books of English Literature. For the use of High Schools, for Private Students, and for General Readers. By FRANCIS H. UNDERWOOD, A.M. British Authors; Cloth, $2.50. American Authors; Cloth, $2.50.

Pronouncing Hand-Book of Three Thousand Words often Mispronounced, and of Words as to which a choice of Pronounciation is allowed. By RICHARD SOULE and LOOMIS J. CAMPBELL. Cloth, 60 cents; School Edition, 35 cents.

Bacon's Essays. With Annotations. By Archbishop WHATELY. Students' Edition, containing a Preface, Notes and a Glossarial Index. By F. F. HEARD. $2.50.

Art; its Laws and the Reasons for Them. Collected, considered and arranged for General and Educational purposes. By SAMUEL P. LONG. $2.00.

Manual of Bible Selections and Responsive Exercises. For Public and Private Schools of all grades, Sabbath and Mission, and Reform Schools, and Family Worship. By Mrs. S. B. PERRY. $1.00.

The Art of Projecting. By Prof. A. E. DOLBEAR. A Manual of Experimentation in Physics, Chemistry and Natural History, with the Porte-Lumière and Magic Lantern. With numerous Illustrations. $1.50.

The Telephone. By Prof. A. E. DOLBEAR. An account of the Phenomena of Electricity, Magnetism and Sound. Illustrated. 75 cents.

Arithmetic for Young Children. By HORACE GRANT. American Edition, edited by WILLARD SMALL. Cloth, 35 cents.

A Manual of English Pronounciation and Spelling. Containing Alphabetical Vocabulary of the Language. By R. SOULE and W. A. WHEELER. $1.50.

Works of Virgil. Translated into English Prose, with an Essay on the English Translators of Virgil, by Prof. JOHN CONINGTON, late of Oxford University. Edited by JOHN ADDINGTON SYMONDS. Cloth, $2.00.

A Selection of English Synonymes. By Archbishop WHATELY. $1.00.

Latin School Series. Selections from Latin Classic Authors. With Notes and a Vocabulary. By FRANCIS GARDNER, A. M. GAY and A. H. BUCK, Masters of the Boston Latin School.
Phœdrus, Justin, Nepos. $1.25.
Cæsar, Curtius, Ovid. $1.50.

Getting to Paris. A Book of Practical French Conversation. By FRANCIS S. WILLIAMS, A.M. $1.50. Same in two parts; each, $1.00.

The Historical Student's Manual. By ALFRED WAITES. 8vo. Cloth, 75 cents.

Mother-Play. By FREDERICK FROEBEL. Translated from the German by Miss JARVIS and Miss DWIGHT. With 50 full-page Illustrations, and a number of German Kindergarten songs with English words. $2.00.

Reminiscences of Froebel. By Baroness MARENHOLTZ-BUELOW. Translated by Mrs. HORACE MANN. With a Biographical Sketch of Froebel.—By Miss EMILY SHIREFF. $1.50.

Primer of Design. By CHARLES A. BARRY. 75 cents net; by mail, 90 cents.

Model and Object Drawing. By CHARLES A. BARRY. 50 cents.

⁎ Sold by all Booksellers and sent postpaid on receipt of price. Special Terms to Schools and Teachers.

LEE AND SHEPARD, Publishers, Boston.

HIGGINSON'S SHORT STUDIES
—OF—
AMERICAN AUTHORS.
Cloth, 75 Cents.

EXCERPTS FROM THE PRESS.

ROOM FOR ONE MORE,
By Mary Thacher Higginson.

16mo, Cloth, Illustrated, $1.25.

₄ Sold by all Booksellers, and sent postpaid on receipt of price.

LEE AND SHEPARD. Publishers, Boston.

HIGGINSON'S WORKS.

I.

OUT-DOOR PAPERS. 16mo. $1.50.

"That wise and gracious Bible of physical education." — PROF. M. C. TYLER, *in Brownville Papers.*
"The chapters on 'Water-Lilies,' 'The Life of Birds,' and 'The Procession of Flowers' are charming specimens of a poetic faculty in description, combined with a scientific observation and analysis of nature." — *London Patriot.*

II.

MALBONE: AN OLDPORT ROMANCE. 16mo. $1.50.

"As a 'romance' it seems to us the most brilliant that has appeared in this country since Hawthorne (whom the author in some points has the happiness to resemble) laid down the most fascinating pen ever held by an American author." — JOHN G. SAXE.

III.

ARMY LIFE IN A BLACK REGIMENT. 16mo. $1.50.

"His narratives of his works and adventures in 'The Atlantic Monthly' attracted general attention by their graphic humor and their picturesque and poetical descriptions." — *London Spectator.*

IV.

ATLANTIC ESSAYS. 12mo. $1.50.

"A book which will most assuredly help to raise the standard of American literature. Mr. Higginson's own style is, after Hawthorne's, the best which America has yet produced. He possesses simplicity, directness, and grace. We must strongly recommend this volume of essays, not to be merely read, but to be studied. It is as sound in substance as it is graceful in expression." — *Westminster Review.*

V.

OLDPORT DAYS. *With 10 Heliotype Illustrations.* 12mo. $2.00.

"Mr. Higginson's 'Oldport Days' have an indescribable charm. The grace and refinement of his style are exquisite. His stories are pleasant; his pictures of children and his talk about them are almost pathetic in their tenderness: but in his descriptions of nature he is without a rival." — *Boston Daily Advertiser.*

SHORT STUDIES OF AMERICAN AUTHORS. Reprinted from "The Literary World."

ROOM FOR ONE MORE. A STORY FOR CHILDREN. By MARY THACHER HIGGINSON.

LEE & SHEPARD, Publishers, Boston